I0623010

BADLANDS

LUCAS PEDERSON

SEVERED PRESS
HOBART TASMANIA

BADLANDS

1

The dead man stumbled through the sand, and the Bounty Hunter took aim.

A damn long trek through the dense forests of Wyoming and Northern Colorado, but now, the rotten bastard was done. No more fight left in him. It would ring up a better price if the orncry pig was brought in alive.

But the Bounty Hunter didn't play games.

He squeezed the revolver's trigger and the dead man dropped, face first, into the sand.

Above, a buzzard made a raspy caw. Goddamn things were always about.

The Bounty Hunter holstered his six-shooter, adjusted his black hat, and walked over to the dead man. A hole in the back of his head welled with blood. The Bounty Hunter kicked the dead man over. Officially dead. He had let bounties live before, though killed them in the end. They didn't know how to behave, even if they knew they should. After a few of those, the Bounty Hunter decided it wasn't worth it and shot the bastards.

He didn't have time for bullshit these days.

The Bounty Hunter tied a rope around the dead man's legs and dragged him through the sand while the wicked desert sun lashed down at him like fiery whips. Truth be told, he despised the West. He loathed the heat and the people. Even the very air angered him.

He came from the northern Iowa Territory, but the West was where the money was. Money he needed for back home. Although a home he hadn't returned to in far too many years.

After a while of dragging the dead man through the desert, the Bounty Hunter stopped and lit a nub of a rolled cigarette. His last. Celebrating, he told himself while scanning the barren landscape. The trek back to his horse would be a tough one, but five hundred dollars was worth the struggle. They were somewhere in the Arizona Territory and Sheriff Jones was in Silver Runs, Arizona. Roughly northeast, the Bounty Hunter reckoned.

He dragged the dead man through the sand.

The buzzards rasped and cawed at him. Two…now three. Somehow the bastards knew when something just died. Smell of blood, maybe?

The Bounty Hunter grunted and thought, *More like dumb luck.*

Regardless, one thing could be counted on in the West: death was lucrative for both critters and men. The Bounty Hunter wiped sweat away from his face with a grimy, calloused hand. He puffed out his cheeks in a heavy sigh and spat out the remains of the cigarette. He squinted at the shimmering heat wavering a few inches above the tawny sand in the horizon.

Rope over his right shoulder, grunting while the weight seemed to grow more and more, he dragged the dead man along.

He couldn't go on like this for long. Sooner or later, the heat would stop him dead. Many people died that way. Even from the Iowa Territory, he knew what the heat could do. Farming in such heat killed a couple of friends he had growing up. Not enough water, he assumed. Or, perhaps, people worked themselves literally to death sometimes. Because only two laws made sense for farmers. Produce and profit. All too many failed at profit, even if they fed the region.

Sometimes, folks died of starvation, regardless.

Hunting helped, but, eventually, some people just weren't built for the Iowa Territory. All that vast prairie land…

So overwhelming. Much like the desert lands of the southwest had been overwhelming for him in the beginning. There was life in the desert lands, though not enough for a person to survive more than a couple of days. You could cut open a cactus for water…when there were cactuses around. Now, however, while he grunted and pulled, as the rope dug into his shoulder and the sweat trickled into his eyes, there were no cactuses. There wasn't any greenery. Nothing but vast, tawny sand.

The Bounty Hunter's pale, blue eyes squinted at the horizon. He ignored the trickle of sweat squiggling down his tanned, lined face. He ignored the stink of the body he dragged, as well as his own. A bath. Yes. A bath would be most important once the dead man was delivered. And he hated to think what the dead man would smell like by then. There were quite a few miles between the desert and Silver Runs.

"Ya ain't gonna make it, Hunter," a craggy voice whispered.

The Bounty Hunter stopped, heart thudding heavily. He glanced around, but there was no one else. No one, except for the dead man. The Bounty Hunter grunted, though looked at the dead man anyway. Somewhere in his middle twenties, the Bounty Hunter assumed, though appeared older with all the scars. He reckoned the sheriff knew his true age, or close enough. And, honestly, it didn't matter.

What mattered was the five hundred dollars he could send to the Iowa Territory.

What mattered was…who spoke to him just now? He had never heard voices before. So. who…

The dead man chuckled, though his face never moved; nor did his mouth.

"Heat's gettin' to ya, Hunter. Hearin' things, I s'pose. Seen it enough in my day. I reckon ya ain't got long."

The lines at the corners of his eyes deepened like dark slits when the Bounty Hunter frowned. He shook his head and continued dragging the dead man. Stopping wasn't a good idea in the desert. As for the dead man's voice? He reckoned it was just the heat playing tricks, as it was wont to do. He needed to get out of this Hell before it captured him. Before it first drove him mad, then killed him.

A raspy chuckle lifted behind him. "Ya bit off more than ya could chew here, Hunter. Y'er not gonna make it. You'll be jus' like me soon enough."

"Fuck off," the Bounty Hunter said, glare focused on the wavering horizon. His blue eyes never wavered.

The voice wasn't real. It couldn't be real. The dead man was dead. The hole in the back of the outlaw's head said so.

Just the heat, he thought.

"Might as well jus' stop now. Ya won't make it outta Hell's sandbox. No one this far in ever makes it out."

The Bounty Hunter said nothing, gaze fixed on the horizon. The sun beat on him with fiery fists. The buzzards cawed and shrieked at him. He didn't look up to count them, but watched their shadows circling above him on the sand. The old, worn leather of his boots creaked and groaned around his feet. He kicked himself for not buying a new pair before taking after the dead man.

He blamed Sheriff Jones for that. The old bastard was chomping at the bit like breaking in a horse. Wanted the dead man, who went by the name of John Wynne, to be brought in, dead or alive, in a week. An impossible feat, for most.

For the Bounty Hunter, a minor irritation.

Or so he thought at first.

The dead man, or rather, John, had turned out to be a great deal more than just a minor irritation, however. Indeed, he became a goddamn cunning son of a bitch. Evaded the Bounty Hunter more than once, especially in Colorado. Almost lost him there. The hunt took longer than any other in the Bounty Hunter's memory.

Bounty Hunter.

Well, that's what he was now. Perhaps next week he would be a gunslinger, or assassin, or whatever title would be bestowed upon him while he gathered money and sent it back home for his daughter. He was whoever anyone needed him to be. He was a man with no name in the West, and he preferred it that way.

He longed for the day when they had enough money and—

Was the dead man heavier now? More strain on the rope digging into his shoulder. He cocked his hat back a bit, wiped sweat away from his eyes and glanced over his shoulder.

A buzzard, dark beak dripping with the dead man's blood, shrieked at him. It must have landed on the corpse while he was sifting through his thoughts. Shirt torn, a splash of red across the dead man's chest.

The Bounty Hunter dropped the rope, pulled his revolver, swung around and fired. The force of the bullet plucked the old ugly buzzard off the corpse. It gave a raspy cry and flopped around on the ground before finally falling still. The Bounty Hunter holstered his gun, picked the rope up and dragged the dead man through the desert.

A rough chuckle rose, followed by the dead man's voice. "Ya won't make it, Hunter. Ya won't. Yonder buzzards'll be eatin' *you* next."

But the Bounty Hunter, or so he came to be this time around, shook his head and ventured on through the sand. Voices of the dead be damned. Buzzards with bloody beaks, be damned. He needed to keep moving. Keep his focus on the shimmering horizon. A deceptive horizon promising water. The death of many who pursued the mirage without thought. Thirst was a strong motivator.

As it was now.

The Bounty Hunter's throat ached for the cool flow of water and the ache in his stomach to fade. To feel okay again. Or, at least, okay enough to live.

How long had it been since he had a drink of water? How long before entering the desert? He couldn't remember. Nor could he rightly remember how long he'd been chasing the dead man into the desert. Not a day's worth, but close? Maybe.

His heart thudded heavily. He shook his head, trying to clear the cotton clouding his mind. It worked, for a short time, anyway. He swallowed and his throat gave a dry click. His lips crackled like old snakeskin when he grimaced from an ache in his gut.

He needed water.

A need more than a thought. Something essential to surviving. Mayhap the most import thing.

Water.

Above, the sun clawed at him and the buzzards screamed. Death, plus one. One would claim him, the other would feed off him.

He staggered, shook his head, and continued onward.

Still, he dragged the dead man through the sand. Because he had to. Because, if he let his fears take over, he'd be dead, and his little girl would be put in some orphanage or another once the money he sent dried up. Dying be damned, all that mattered in such a brutal world, was her. Then again, if he died, the money would stop. Her caregiver might pull up stakes and leave her to rely on her wits to survive.

A fifty-fifty chance.

A chance the Bounty Hunter wasn't willing to take.

The sand eventually gave way to scraggly weeds and small clusters of cactuses. Signs of life. He tried to swallow, but his throat was dry. His tongue felt like a thick chunk of moldy cloth. That's also when he realized he had stopped sweating. His heart thrummed and his stomach ached. The muscles down his back and legs quivered and burned.

The Bounty Hunter staggered forward, vision blurring in and out. He squinted and smiled. His chapped lips cracked open in several spots, oozing blood.

He fell to his knees in the sand and pursed his bleeding lips in a whistle.

He blew a breath, though wasn't sure if a sound came out. The Bounty Hunter staggered a few steps then swayed. His head throbbed. Dizzy, he squinted ahead. Nothing. More desert. More sand. Nothing. It was hopeless. It…

A low chuckle filled his head. "Ahhh, look at ya now. 'Bout ready to keel over, ain't ya? Ah, revenge is sweet. Ain't it sweet?" The dead man chuckled again.

A growl rumbled deep in the Bounty Hunter's throat. His vision, like the sharp tip of a dagger, stabbed the horizon. The dizziness subsided a bit, though did not go away. He stood and staggered forward. His right boot kicked up a small spray of sand. The horizon itself was too blurry to make out, but there was green in all that blur. Green meant trees. Trees meant shade. They also marked the spot where he tied his horse up. A nice grassy spot for Warlock.

Warlock had been his horse for a good three years. A fine black and white paint horse the Bounty Hunter won in a duel over, of all things, a shot of whiskey. The West was not only dangerous, but also utterly ridiculous at times. Apparently, a shot of whiskey meant more than a shot of whiskey. It meant life or death, and possessions. It was another thing the Bounty Hunter hated about the West. The abundant hypocrisies. The Iowa Territory had its fair share, but the West and South West…holy shit. He heard about the southeast of the nation and refused to even venture that way. Whatever the cost.

The Bounty Hunter shuffled through the sand until his worn boots scuffed denser weeds. He listened to the weeds whisper over his jeans. His head was like a bowl of water sloshing from side to side. Ahead—twelve feet? Twenty? Three?—he thought he saw something move in all the blurriness. Warlock? He tried to whistle again and like before couldn't be sure if he was actually whistling or not. If so, the figure in front of him didn't move. It didn't give Warlock's usual chuff. Nothing but the sound of a mild breeze sighing through the weeds.

No. It wouldn't be Warlock. He was tied to a tree. Also, if tied to a tree, how could he come running anyway?

The Bounty Hunter shook his head. This man with no name—as he liked it—in the southwest. As a man with a daughter to think of and support. A daughter he would rather be planting beans or corn with on the farm than gunslinging.

Maybe, if he made enough money, they could do just that.

For now, however…

He meant to ask who was standing in front of him, but all that came out was a dry growl. Something ugly he didn't like at all. Something…not human.

The Bounty Hunter stopped and dropped the rope. His right hand drifted toward the sandalwood butt of his revolver. The growling stopped and the Bounty Hunter swayed. He couldn't help it. His body paid no mind to his brain. Weariness stole over him in massive, gray waves. His knees quivered, threatening to buckle. Somewhere, not far, a buzzard cried.

The dark figure, some hunched thing, almost human-like, lurched closer. That papery growl grew a bit louder. A sound which drove a thin, cold spike deeper and deeper into his stomach. A sound that might very well drive him mad.

It darted forward.

The Bounty Hunter drew his revolver and shot the creature. It whirled away with a blood chilling shriek. He squinted, trying to see what the thing could be, but his vision failed him. Everything was blurry and in shades of gray, speckled with white. Only thing that came close to what he was experiencing was the time in the hayloft slinging bales until he buckled. Everything went gray and he later woke up in his bed with Mom dabbing a cool rag on his forehead.

Overheated, was what Mom told him. Being too hot and not drinking enough water. Not enough breaks. For that, the Bounty Hunter blamed his father. The man would sit on his tractor and bark while slurping water from his leather canteen. Not once would Father offer a drink.

Such was the way in the Iowa Territory. A place where only the strong survived, according to his father. Something that made sense at first, then, later, the Bounty Hunter discarded. Because, sometimes, it was the strong who must protect and lift up the weak. There was no reason to stamp the weaker folks down. And where they might be weaker in body, their minds could be vast and beautiful. It wasn't exactly his father's fault. The man had never expanded his horizons. He didn't venture far from the farm or the twenty acres of land. The people he knew were the people he knew from when he was a child.

No diversity.

Now, the Bounty Hunter drooped, his arm too weak to lift the revolver. He squinted at the dark figure while it appeared to sink to the ground. He tried lifting his arm to aim the revolver, but it was like his arm didn't exist anymore.

He dropped to his knees and the dark figure rose to its feet.

No. No. He couldn't die now. His little girl was counting on him. He needed to…

He fell forward and his world blacked out before his face hit the ground.

2

Cold…

Something cold dripped onto his forehead. So soothing, he wanted to stay wherever he was forever. A gentle hum echoed in his ears. Low and beautiful in tone.

The dripping stopped, and for a moment, he almost lost all hope it would ever return. Then it did and everything was alright again. He floated in gray waters, unable to move.

After some time, he let the cool dripping and beautiful humming lull him back to sleep.

***

It was the tapping that woke him.

His eyelids fluttered a second or two before opening. He squinted into dim light and groaned. He rolled onto his back and blinked at a dark ceiling. Stone? A cave? He shook his head and rolled onto his left side away from the light.

The Bounty Hunter swallowed and grimaced at the tenderness of his throat.

He had some kind of throat problem when he was younger. Something the doctor called pus throat and would later be termed as strep throat. An illness attacked the throat. Made it painful to swallow. Like jagged knife blades slicing up and down his throat, cutting it to ribbons. Shredding it to oblivion.

This wasn't exactly like that, but close. It hurt well enough, and he reckoned he needed to find some water, yet…

Where am I?

The Bounty Hunter opened his eyes again and squinted into a gloom not quite dark. There was just enough light for his sight to adjust a bit. Dim, though highlighted by the pale sun at his back. His gaze slipped over a ragged rock wall and peculiar carvings. Old carvings, he reckoned.

"How do you feel?"

The voice bounced off the stone walls for a moment before fading. *A cave*, he thought.

At first, he didn't answer. He just laid there on his side and stared at the oddly beautiful carving of what appeared to be a buffalo. He didn't know they roamed this far southwest, which intrigued the Bounty Hunter. If buffalo roamed this far southwest, everything he knew about the animal was wrong.

"I know you are awake."

The Bounty Hunter sighed. He rolled onto his back, tried to sit, but about halfway, his head swam in throbbing, gray sludge and he needed to lay back down again.

"You are not ready." A pause. A gentle hand slipped around the back of his head, lifting it. "Here…drink."

His caretaker, or whoever the person might be, sounded like a man, though his English was slow and broken. Someone just learning. His heart stuttered. Could it be an Apache? Navajo? He didn't know. Some were more aggressive than others, and rightfully so. White men were trying to steal their land. No different than some outlaws robbing a bank or trying to overtake a small farm. Land was a valuable thing, but it was also spiritual and sentimental. A way of life. One is always attached to some land or another. The very spirt of the earth, mayhap.

Was his caretaker an ally or were there more ominous intentions? He had heard of cannibals in the south. But, maybe, that was more toward the east? He couldn't remember. He reckoned there were cannibals everywhere.

His hand crept to his left revolver. He played, draw, roll, shoot, through his mind. It would have to be quick and hit the mark or he would be dead. Shoot first, because one could never trust in such brutal lands. It was, as far as the Bounty Hunter came to think about it, an every-man-for-himself land.

He moved just enough for his hand to curl around the butt of his gun. All he needed to do was count to three and—

"I will not hurt," the person paused a moment and followed with more emphasis, "I will *not*...hurt *you*."

But the Bounty Hunter didn't believe the other person. Trusting someone, anyone, in these parts came at a price. And, often, that price was the ultimate one.

One he could not afford.

One he almost paid out there in the desert.

Despite what the other person said, he drew the revolver, rolled and—

A bare-chested man whacked the gun from the Bounty Hunter's hand before he could squeeze the trigger. Something that had never happened before. He didn't even see where the gun landed. He went for the knife in his boot, but the stranger yanked his arm up and twisted it in a painful, unnatural angle.

He cried out and tried to land a punch with his free hand.

The stranger caught it and twisted that arm too.

With a dry growl, the Bounty Hunter tried to overpower the other man, though to no avail.

"Stop. Please." The stranger's voice was near to pleading. "I will not hurt you."

The Bounty Hunter stopped struggling. He was turned away from the stranger. "Who—Who are you?" His voice was a crackly, raspy mess. He barely recognized himself.

"Coy Wolf," the man said.

He released the Bounty Hunter and gently turned him around. The Bounty Hunter blinked at the man hunkered in front of him. A native. Apache, perhaps, though he doubted it. They were too far south for one thing. Another, the man's brown eyes were too mellow. His heavily lined face...too gentle. Not just for Apache, but in general. It had been a long time since he saw such a gentle expression. Last time, as far as he could remember, was a good two years ago.

Older black man. One of the rare free slaves in the area. A man who no doubt fought his entire life and finally owned his own store of goods, living the rest of his days in relative peace. His little shop sold jerky, candies, rice, flour, and sugar, for the most part. Up yonder in Colorado, that had been. A man who saw and lived horrors beyond anything the Bounty Hunter could imagine. Still, when he went into the store to get some jerky before setting out on a different hunt, the man gave the entire building a certain warmth, even above the gentle heat given to the place by a single potbelly stove.

He rocked in an elderly wooden rocking chair that had to be as old as him, if not a few years more. The man smiled while the Bounty Hunter browsed the small shop. They were the only two in the building. Outside, winter was just kicking autumn out on its ass. Even in the warm shop there were twinges of cold here and there, despite how well sealed the store appeared to be. You could build the greatest home, and still, the cold would find its way in. Living in the Iowa Territory, the Bounty Hunter knew the cold well enough.

The entire time the Bounty Hunter browsed, the old black man smiled. Kindness radiated from him and he didn't say a word until the Bounty Hunter plopped a two-pound bag of rice on the counter and asked for two pounds of jerky.

The old man snorted, stood from the rocking chair without a wobble or sway and gracefully strode across the shop to the counter.

"Y'want wide or thin?" the old man asked, opening a sack. He still held the gentle, kind expression on his wrinkled face.

The Bounty Hunter smiled some. "Never thought about it before. What do you recommend?"

"Ah," the old man said, sliding open a glass door to the assortment of jerky. "Y'new 'round these parts. Well, lemme show ya." He brought out two separate strips of jerky. One was about four inches wide, while the other was nearly two inches.

The Bounty Hunter chose the four-inch wide and when the sack was tied, he paid.

Before the Bounty Hunter stepped through the door into the bitter evening, the old black man said, "Your reasons are y'own. Not a man should be judged, but I see much turmoil in you. A man with so much turmoil is like a keg of gunpowder." He carefully lowered himself into the rocking chair. "All ya need is a spark."

The Bounty Hunter, not sure what to say, thanked the man and left.

He was never able to return and often wondered what became of the old man. He thought about that kind face, those gentle eyes, every day.

The same face, those same eyes, fell on him now. A native, yes, but of which tribe? And did it really matter? The man said he was safe, but could it all be a trick?

Questions without answers.

The more he gazed upon the stranger, however, the more the Bounty Hunter noticed the red gouge along the right side of the man's face. It cut all the way into the thick salt and pepper mane of hair.

The man must have noticed the Bounty Hunter looking and smiled. "You almost missed."

The Bounty Hunter relaxed a bit. Not fully, because the man could attack at any time. "What do you want?"

"To help," Coy Wolf said.

"I almost killed you."

After a second or two, the man nodded. "But you did not."

"Okay. So, what do you want?"

Coy Wolf, who might have been in his middle sixties, smiled. "To help." He turned away, and when he faced the Bounty Hunter again, he held a small, clay bowl filled with water.

The Bounty Hunter thought about going for his other gun and dismissed the urge. He was too weak. Too slow. The other man would end him before he could so much as reach for the revolver. And that was another thing. He still carried his guns. If this was a way to capture and kill, then why did the man leave the guns in their holsters?

The answer was simple and one he should have seen sooner.

The man was, indeed, trying to help. The Bounty Hunter, being too thick headed, hadn't realized it. Even now, he questioned the man's motives.

"Where's my horse?" the Bounty Hunter croaked.

The man smiled, turned a bit and nodded toward the mouth of the cave. "In shade. Fed her grass and roots."

The Bounty Hunter relaxed some more. It could all be a trick, but he didn't think so. Knowing how to tell when a person was lying was one of his talents. There were signs and Coy Wolf revealed none of them.

The man held the clay bowl of water out toward the Bounty Hunter. "Drink. Slow."

The Bounty Hunter's throat ached for the water. His body quaked in anticipation. He took the bowl in trembling hands and brought the brim to his lips. Lips which cracked and split open painfully when he pursed to drink. The pain was a small annoyance. His entire body quivered when the cool water touched those bleeding lips, shook when it filled his dry mouth and trickled down his throat as he swallowed.

The first sip ignited a desire, an essential and immediate need, so strong he couldn't stop himself from upending the bowl and chugging the water.

"Ah-ah," the other man said and yanked the bowl away from the Bounty Hunter.

The Bounty Hunter lunged for it, but the man was still much too quick and backed away before his hands could latch onto the bowl.

Coy Wolf stood and shook his head. His face had grown from gentle to stern. Silvery black eyebrows knitted together in a frown.

"Too fast," the man said. "Get sick."

The Bounty Hunter's jaw clenched. The man was right. He hadn't drunk water for God knew how long. He about died of thirst. Like when he about died of the same thing in the hayloft so long ago. Even his mother told him not to drink too fast or he'd throw up.

So, the Bounty Hunter sighed and tried to relax. Though his gaze never strayed too far from the bowl of water.

The other man placed the bowl on a ledge cut out from a stone wall above what appeared to be a fireplace. The clay gave a sharp click against the stone which echoed throughout the small cave. Small, as far as the Bounty Hunter could tell, anyway.

He opened his mouth to ask when he'd get another drink, but the other man held up a silencing hand.

"Who…is the man?"

The Bounty Hunter blinked. "I don't—"

The other man ran a thumb across his throat. A bit alarmed, the Bounty Hunter wasn't sure how to respond.

Then it all finally clicked together.

"You mean the dead man."

The native nodded.

The Bounty Hunter grunted. "He was a bad man. Killed an entire family, six children. Killed many others before that. I was hired to bring him in."

The other man nodded, though with his distant expression, the Bounty Hunter wasn't sure how much he actually understood.

"Why kill him?"

The Bounty Hunter shrugged. "Because I was tired of chasing him. Been two months. Long time for me."

Coy Wolf sighed and crossed his arms over his chest. He wore a tattered gray shirt, split open down the front and frayed pants made of patched together cloth or canvas. His feet were bare and were likely heavily calloused.

"To kill a...killer..." Coy Wolf said. "You are not a god."

The Bounty Hunter shrugged. "No. I'm not. But it was either stop him or chase him deeper into the desert." He pointed at the bowl of water. "I need more, I reckon."

The other man smiled. "Yes. Are you a bad man?" He brought the bowl of water over and handed it to the Bounty Hunter.

He could have lied, of course. He could have said he was a lawman, of all things, but instead he said, "I reckon some might think I am."

Coy Wolf, face solemn, nodded. He didn't say anything and instead picked up the Bounty Hunter's revolver.

The Bounty Hunter watched the man over the brim of the bowl as he drank. His body tensed, like a compressed spring. Ready to blast into action if need be.

All unfounded, however, as the man brought the gun over and gently placed it beside the Bounty Hunter and walked off toward the mouth of the cave. Trusting, the older man. One thing the Bounty Hunter had written into his internal laws was: Never turn your back on a stranger, no matter how friendly they appeared.

The Bounty Hunter lowered the bowl, now empty, and said, "Do you live here alone?"

The man stopped just inside the mouth of the cave. He did not look at the Bounty Hunter when he spoke. "Yes. I am…" He shook his head, obviously trying to pronounce the right words. "I am…*outcast.*"

The Bounty Hunter scooted back, resting his back against the cool, stone wall. "Outcast?"

"Yes." Coy Wolf lowered his head. "I did not fit in."

This piqued the Bounty Hunter's interest. It was not often a native was found without a tribe. "Which tribe are you—"

"Comanche," Coy Wolf said and leaned against the inside of the cave's opening. His head remained lowered.

Comanche…

The most feared tribe in the region. Not because they were evil, but because they didn't take any shit and fought back against the white man. The Bounty Hunter respected them. He also feared them. As many did. They were a force to be reckoned with.

And, yet, Coy Wolf appeared to be the complete opposite. There was nothing aggressive about the older man. No signs of hate or fear. Only calm. Indeed, the man appeared sad. He lifted his head and stared out through the mouth of the cave. The sunlight barely trickled in and the Bounty Hunter assumed it must be near dark. Dusk flirting with its old friend, night once more.

"We are proud people," Coy Wolf said. "Not evil. We wish…to keep our ways. Not yours."

The Bounty Hunter nodded. This was the first time really speaking with a Comanche. First time he'd spoken more than a few passing words to a native, for that matter. He was just, typically, a man on a mission. He rarely even talked to white folk. His mission was simple, and he didn't care to make friends. What mattered was his daughter. He was only in the West for her. The money. Build up a saving and never worry about anything ever again. Build a cabin out of town. Farm for a living when the money began drying up. If he couldn't send enough to be saved for a lifetime. That was the plan, anyway.

However, plans always changed, as he was coming to discover. Who knew what the next day, let alone next hour would bring?

Coy Wolf straightened, sighed and faced the Bounty Hunter. He was a little more than a silhouette cast from the opening of the cave. "Time for fire."

The man moved so gracefully toward the fireplace dug into the wall of the cave, the Bounty Hunter hardly had time to register Coy before the sparks sprayed onto a pile of kindling. Clumped under the tented kindling was what appeared to be gray moss. The light was failing, so the Bounty Hunter wasn't so sure what exactly the clump was. He shifted, slid the revolver Coy Wolf returned to him into its holster and tried to ignore the grumbling of his hungry belly.

"There is a story," Coy Wolf said when the moss caught flame. He fanned the flames a bit, and the fire spread to the kindling. He added more kindling. "Elder spoke of it...many times." The flames rose and crackled throughout the cave. Their orange light flickered along the ragged walls and ceiling.

"Once," Coy said, "there was a boy...and coyote. Boy did not like coyote. Coyote...he steals food from family. Boy...hunts coyote to kill her. No more stealing. His family is hungry."

Coy placed a thicker stick on the growing fire. Embers swirled up and disappeared.

Must be a chimney of some sort in there, the Bounty Hunter thought.

"The boy," Coy continued, "hunted coyote for…many days. On the last day, he found coyote with deer leg…it…stole from boy's family. The boy drew his bow. Arrow aimed at coyote."

Coy shook his head and placed another length of wood on the fire. "The boy did not notice. The coyote had many pups before he released the arrow." Coy lowered his head. "Too late…as boy wished…to take back arrow. Too late. When boy knelt …coyote told him she was sorry. She says, 'Was just feeding my young.' The boy looked at the pups crying in their den."

The Bounty Hunter blinked for the first time since Coy Wolf began the little story. "And?"

Coy grunted, and placed more wood on the growing fire. "No and. End of story." He stood and gestured to the fire. "Put wood on. I will be back."

The Bounty Hunter frowned, though said nothing and watched Coy walk out of the cave. The man soon disappeared not far from the opening. The Bounty Hunter fought to stand, though managed. His head was a swarm of deadly hornets he mentally batted away until his gaze fixed on the bowl of water on the mantel above the dugout fireplace.

He made it to the mantel and brought the bowl to his lips and drank the rest of the water. Which wasn't much. He hunkered down in front of the fire, curious. As he suspected, there was a rather large hole, which appeared natural, cut through the charred stone. The way it was positioned it seemed the makeshift chimney led toward the mouth of the cave. The more the Bounty Hunter strolled the cave the more he realized Coy had been living here a long time and figured out all the tricks. The man created a home out of stone. There was even a solid door for the narrow mouth of the cave. There were deep grooves in the floor and ceiling where the door slid into.

The Bounty Hunter smiled at the creativity of it all. Likewise, Coy's bed was carved into a wall not far from where the Bounty Hunter woke up. An elongated hole that went about four feet in by at least seven feet long. There were several skins of various animal pelts piled on the inventive bed, along with a hefty old quilt.

"Wife made the quilt," Coy spoke, startling the Bounty Hunter. He hadn't heard the man return.

The Bounty Hunter, shaking off how quiet the native man's footsteps were, nodded. "Looks like great care was taken."

Coy stepped around the Bounty Hunter. His heavily calloused hand scratched over the fabric. A smile touched his lips. "Made for our child." He sighed, straightened and faced the Bounty Hunter. "Time to eat." Coy wiped tears from his cheeks, and walked toward the fireplace.

A frown fell over the Bounty Hunter's face. "Where is—"

"Gone." Coy pulled the skin of a rattlesnake off and gutted the thing faster than anyone the Bounty Hunter knew. "All gone."

The Bounty Hunter lowered his head, heart aching for Coy. There was no need to give Coy condolences, even if the Bounty Hunter wanted to. The man was haunted by ghosts, that much was clear. Regardless, Coy might take offence to condolences. So, the Bounty Hunter let the subject fall to the wayside and joined the man who saved him by the fire while Coy cut and skewered the rattlesnake meat.

"Tomorrow," Coy said, propping the meat over the flames, "you will have strength to go."

"Thank you," the Bounty Hunter said. He sat down beside the other man. "You saved my life."

Coy waved a dismissive hand. "We are all life. Life is for—*give*ness. We are life. We are chaos."

That last held the Bounty Hunter in sway for a second or two.

We are chaos...

Nothing before now, besides his daughter, made sense until Coy Wolf spoke those words. People were, indeed, chaos. And they could not be stopped. Some, he reckoned, wouldn't care anyway. If one was different, they became the enemy. As sickening as it was, such were the times. And, in the Bounty Hunter's experience, people rarely changed...

The Bounty Hunter didn't bother Coy further. The gratitude, he hoped, was received. Coy's response, although thoughtful, didn't quite fit with giving or accepting thanks. Rather, Coy gave a broad response to people in general.

So, he waited, savoring the sweet smell while the rattlesnake cooked.

Once the rattlesnake was ready, Coy slid a section off into the Bounty Hunter's hands. It was hot. Sizzling. He tossed the rattlesnake meat from hand to hand until it cooled enough to handle and eat.

Coy snorted, brought his own chunk of meat to his mouth and bit in. Clear juices trickled down his chin while he chewed. Undaunted by any burning. The Bounty Hunter found himself gaping in disbelief.

Finally, he swallowed a mouthful of snake and said, "How did you not burn your mouth?"

The other man smiled and popped a small piece into his mouth. He chewed, swallowed. "It was not so hot." He pointed at the skewer of meat, which rested on a clean slab of stone and grinned at the Bounty Hunter. "I let mine cool like smart person."

It took the Bounty Hunter a few seconds to realize Coy Wolf had just made a joke. Maybe not the funniest, but the Bounty Hunter chuckled all the same. How long had it been since he laughed? How long since he heard a joke? Especially one as pure as Coy's? Far too long, he reckoned.

Coy grinned and sank his teeth into another chunk of meat.

The Bounty Hunter, still chuckling, pulled more food off the skewer and ate.

They didn't speak until the entire rattlesnake was finished.

Soon enough, they sat with bowls of water from a nearby spring Coy collected for them. He helped Coy slide the heavy wooden door into place at the mouth of the cave. In the fireplace, red coals winked at them. The entire place eased into a peaceful twilight. Coy made no move to place more wood on the coals to get the fire going again. Instead, he nodded at the Bounty Hunter.

"Buried the man you killed."

A sliver of anger slipped under the proverbial thick skin blanketing his emotions. His jaw clenched. His right hand slid to the butt of the revolver on his hip.

Coy's gaze followed the Bounty Hunter's every move and smiled. "You can kill me too."

The Bounty Hunter gripped the butt of his gun, body trembling. The man stole his bounty. A large chunk of money which would keep his daughter alive. He…he…

The Bounty Hunter sighed. Even though he still had an urge to rage, he choked it down and said, "As it should be, I reckon."

Coy stared at the dying coals of the fire. "Sometimes we die…to come back better." He looked at the Bounty Hunter. "You are better."

The Bounty Hunter grunted and lowered his head. "No. I'm not."

"There is much strength in you, White Man. All who meet you know this. Saw it the day we met. You are strong and you have a loving heart."

The Bounty Hunter looked away, heart sinking. He shook his head, "You don't know me. You don't know how many I've killed…"

"No," Coy said. "But I see you. I see you without the death. I see a child…"

The Bounty Hunter snapped his gaze back to Coy. "Is that so?"

Coy finished off his bowl of water, stood, and placed it on the outcropped mantel above the fireplace. Before walking off to bed, he said, "Yes. Rest now."

Coy disappeared into the deeper shadows of the cave toward his bed and the Bounty Hunter returned his gaze to the waning coals. Like so many red blinking eyes.

He pulled the few skins Coy put down for him over to the fireplace, found a tattered, brown blanket, and placed a larger chunk of wood on the coals. He wanted the heat to keep the cave warm from the cool desert night. The small log wouldn't do all night, but, maybe, enough for him to fall asleep. The tattered blanket wouldn't do much to fend off the chill, but he had no other choice.

Sacrificing comfort for warmth, he pulled one of the three skins out and used it as a blanket too.

He curled up near the crackling fire, watching the orange, yellow and blue flames dance over the small chunk of wood.

Soon enough, his eyelids drooped.

Soon enough, he knew no more.

3

Beautiful birdsong floated to his ears. Sweet and innocent. The sound of life.

The Bounty Hunter woke, though cringed and tried to hide under the covers from the sunlight spilling into the cave. He was never one to wake late, but his body felt like it was a slab of lard. Weak and unsubstantial. From the mere glimpse of the sun, he guessed it was about midmorning. Near to noon.

From under the covers, he caught the whiff of cooking meat. Not sweet like the rattlesnake, but salty and heavy. Beef? The Bounty Hunter didn't notice any cattle around. If there were, he would've heard them.

"Time to eat," Coy said. "You have a long journey."

Gradually, so not to be blinded by the light, the Bounty Hunter lowered the covers. Coy crouched in front of the fire. The aroma of cooking meat was so strong and savory, the Bounty Hunter absently wiped a runner of drool from his whiskered chin.

Resting on a large slab of flat stone was a loaf of bread and a thick cut of what resembled roast beef. More of the same meat cooked on a spit Coy turned using a long, forked stick every few seconds.

Hot saliva filled the Bounty Hunter's mouth. He swallowed and said, "Looks good."

Coy grunted. "Old pig was too slow. I will cook some and salt the rest."

The Bounty Hunter nodded, broke off a small chunk of bread and popped it into his mouth. It was soft and moist and still warm. He smiled while he chewed. He had forgotten the taste and texture of fresh baked bread. For the meat, he brought out his skinning knife and sliced a piece off the main chunk. It was sweet and salty and perfect. Everything a roasted pig should be. His mind tried to drift to the dead man and what he would tell Sheriff Jones from Silver Runs, and he squashed it quickly.

This moment, right now, all he wanted was to relax and savor good food.

"Water." Coy pointed at the mantel above the fireplace.

The Bounty Hunter brought both bowls down and handed one to Coy. The man nodded, took a sip and placed the water bowl on the slab of stone with the bread and chunk of roasted pig.

Still sizzling, Coy brought down the spit full of meat from notches carved into the stone inside the fireplace. He placed it all on the stone slab while the Bounty Hunter moved the bread and water bowls to make room. The aroma made the Bounty Hunter's stomach grumble. He cut a slice of pig from his chunk and ate it.

Coy smiled while he cut through several large shanks of meat. Carefully, he divided the meat for both of them. The pile in front of the Bounty Hunter made his heart stutter. And, as ravenous as he felt, he wasn't sure he could eat it all.

As though reading his mind, Coy said, "I know ways to save meat if we do not finish."

The Bounty Hunter didn't waste time. He ate almost half of his pile of pig meat and about half the bread. A literal feast. After surviving on beef and buffalo jerky and coffee for so long, a real meal wasn't something to take for granted. So, he ate until he couldn't eat anymore. Full, he waved off anymore Coy offered.

Coy ate less than half the Bounty Hunter and scraped all the leftovers into a large clay bowl.

After breakfast, the Bounty Hunter snugged his hat on as they stepped outside the cave. For the Bounty Hunter, he was captivated by all the green and cactuses surrounding them. Not far, he could have sworn he heard the trickle of water. Coy led the Bounty Hunter's horse, Warlock, around a ragged boulder. The Bounty Hunter smiled and took the reins.

"Good horse," Coy said and sighed. "Be careful on your journeys." He extended a hand. On the calloused palm rested a smooth stone in the shape of a ball. "Luck stone." Coy smiled. "You need it more than me."

The Bounty Hunter chuckled and took the stone from the man's hand. "Many thanks. Would have been a crispy critter out there if not for you."

Coy lowered his head, though didn't say anything.

The Bounty Hunter pocketed the round, white stone and placed a hand on Coy's shoulder. "Well met, my friend."

Coy patted the Bounty Hunter's hand and backed away. "You will do great things, Iowa."

The Bounty Hunter blinked. "How did you know—"

"You speak in your sleep," Coy said and winked. "Do what you must for your daughter. Family is…important."

The Bounty Hunter frowned. "Do you have family?"

Coy looked away. "Yes. They chose to follow the tribe."

"Why didn't you?"

"I…" Coy shook his head and gazed toward the bright horizon. "Sometimes one just cannot."

The Bounty Hunter about asked: Why not? In the end, however, he decided to let it be. He could assume Coy was not like his tribe. Perhaps he thought outside the box or maybe he was smarter. For all he knew, Coy did something awful and was banished. Whatever the case, it didn't matter now.

"Thank you," the Bounty Hunter said before mounting Warlock. The horse shifted and chuffed under him.

"Travel well, Bounty Hunter," Coy said, smiled and walked back to the cave. His home.

The Bounty Hunter tipped his hat, swung Warlock around and instead of heading northeast to Silver Runs, set out for northwest.

He reckoned it was time for some new scenery anyway.

4

He veered away from the desert as much as possible, sticking to the lush green of valleys and scant wooded areas. As he worked his way northwest, he wondered if Sheriff Jones had a bounty on his head yet?

A few times, he stopped to make camp and rest before moving on. There were long, hot days where he would watch his shadow lengthen before the sun dipped below the horizon, and chilly nights sleeping under a vast blanket of stars while the coyotes sang their songs to each other.

He filled his waterskin at every fresh spring he came across and ate his fair share of gristly rabbit and sweet rattlesnake. The journey alone took over twenty days and twenty-one nights before he finally entered a small town called Rucker's Mills. Calling it a town was a stretch, though. More like an upscale village, truth be told. A store for groceries and whatnot. A small bank and stable. A scattering of shacks here and there. The town, however, appeared to be dominated by a massive saloon and hotel. Burned into the wooden sign above the door were the words: CAPTAIN'S REST.

The Bounty Hunter rolled his eyes. He'd seen his fair share of brothels and the Captain's Rest was a brothel. A lot of whorehouses were built above saloons. Not a bad business plan, he supposed. Get the men liquored up and lead them to their rooms...for a price.

Still, he could go for a good stiff drink right now. After everything, a shot of whiskey would be nice. Something to numb the aches and pains, at least for the moment.

He dismounted Warlock and led him to a nearby water trough. He gave his sunburned face and neck a splash of the cool water and let Warlock drink his fill.

Finished, he tied the horse outside Captain's Rest and stepped inside.

The moment the door shut behind him, he was assaulted by the stench of stale cigars, beer and the stink of people. Spoiled onions was the closest analogy he could think of. Unlike most brothels and saloons, there wasn't any music. No piano or fiddle. No singers. Likewise, the few patrons scattered about sat quiet. Where was the shouting and raucous laughter? The spitting. The claps on the back. The card tables overturned by sour losers. The threats and revolvers drawn.

The Captain's Rest appeared to be just that. A place of quiet and rest for people to drown in beer and liquor while their lives slipped slowly away. Maybe even some of them knew it, though the Bounty Hunter reckoned not all did. Sometimes ignorance was bliss. Just as well.

The Bounty Hunter gave the old man with a scraggly gray beard behind the bar a nod. "Whiskey."

Old tender's bushy gray eyebrows knitted together in a frown. "Don' serve drifters here, Mister."

The Bounty Hunter's gaze cut into the old man and to his surprise, the tender did not flinch or look away. A man with steel in his heart. For that, the Bounty Hunter cut the tender some slack and smiled.

"Well, now, would you reckon you'd serve a lawman?" The Bounty Hunter flashed a deputy's star. The original owner of the badge, dead by way of the Bounty Hunter's gun for aiding a train robbery. Not all lawmen were lawful.

The tender's eyes widened and his bushy eyebrows shot up. "Lawman, are ya?" He ducked behind the bar and when he popped back up, he slammed a shot glass and brown bottle down. "Why d'n't ya just say so?"

The Bounty Hunter shrugged. "Been after some bandits. Long ride. Must've slipped my mind."

The tender waved a liver spotted hand at one of the stools in front of the whiskey bottle. "Well met. Drink your fill."

The Bounty Hunter, however, did not take a stool. Instead, he poured his shot of whiskey and leaned against the bar a bit. Not a full lean, because what he learned over the years was to never trust a saloon. Ever. Even if you've visited the same saloon since time out of mind...never trust a saloon and always keep your hand near the butt of your revolver.

The tender smiled, scraggly beard twitching with the effort. "Ya gotta name?"

"Not one I'd give to you, friend."

The tender blinked, perhaps wondering if he'd been insulted or not. In the end, the old man shrugged and went to chat with a couple of other older man down the bar.

The Bounty Hunter sipped his whiskey and shivered when it burned down his throat. He couldn't remember the last bit of whiskey he'd had. If he were to assume...a few months. Now, while the liquor took hold a bit and the next few sips went down without too much burning, he thought about buying a bottle outright and taking it with him. He had no destination in mind but would find work eventually. The West was ripe for outlaws and bounty hunters alike.

The whiskey would help get him through nights when he couldn't sleep too. Although it would dull his senses and in this part of the world one relied on their senses. Even the gut feeling when you felt something wrong, though couldn't see or hear it yet.

No. He would leave without a bottle.

He knocked back the rest of the shot and refilled the glass. His thoughts turned to his daughter, Ana. He sent letters with the money. Just short notes letting Ana know how much he missed her and that he would see her soon.

There were never any letters back because he was never in the same place all the time.

Just need one thousand dollars more, he thought. *Just need a couple of really good jobs and I can—*

"Sheriff Jones said ya might be hard t'find," a grizzled voice rumbled behind the Bounty Hunter. A grunt. "Not for me."

The Bounty Hunter sighed, knocked back his second shot of whiskey and said, "How is the old bastard? Still scratchin' them sores on his face?"

"Payin' me to bring ya in is how he is." The metallic click of a gun hammer being drawn back. "Now, I want ya to put those guns on the bar and turn arou—"

The Bounty Hunter drew his right revolver, spun, and squeezed the trigger in a single motion. The other bounty hunter's head whipped back, a hole the size of a nickel smoldering in the center of his sloped forehead. The man hit the wooden floor like an armload of firewood.

For a moment, he had the attention of the entire saloon. But only for a moment. All those weary, bloodshot eyes soon lowered to whatever thoughts curled in their loathsome minds. A few played cards, though sluggish and dizzy, like old bears waking up after a winter's sleep. Lost. Adrift. Souls without purpose or inspiration. Indeed, there was no light in their eyes. Not even the tender's.

The Bounty Hunter yanked a small pack off the dead man's belt, opened it and dumped all the money inside onto the bar.

The tender frowned.

"For the whiskey." The Bounty Hunter nodded at the dead man. "And coffin." He gave the tender a nod and walked out of Captain's Rest.

Jones already had people after him. And so soon? A double-cross. He'd been played a fool. He yanked

Warlock's reins free and swung onto his horse. Trotted off in one direction, stopped, turned and went another.

Stopped.

Because…how many were after him? Where the hell were they? Sheriff Jones wouldn't just send one, not with the Bounty Hunter's reputation. He wasn't the fastest gunslinger, but he was known. And in the West, if you were known, you could use fear against your enemies better than a bullet. Fear was an immensely powerful thing.

He brought out his compass and turned until he found direct northwest.

It appeared it was off by a few degrees. Maybe that's how the dead man in the saloon found him. Blind luck, more or less.

He couldn't remember what towns or cities lay ahead and it didn't matter. There was a bounty on his head now too.

5

Three days, given the sun and moon.

Three days travel and the only things he encountered were coyotes, rattlesnakes, and the ever-present circling buzzards. Not a soul in sight. The world sifted from desert to green, to desert and back to green again. There never appeared to be much middle ground until he saw the mountains.

He veered farther west. Maybe he'd meet with the ocean. Couldn't be too far, right? Or, perhaps, he would continue in the Northwestern Territories. Hell, why not just keep going until nothing else mattered and life had no meaning except for survival? He imagined himself a bearded, grizzled frontier man. A man who—

"Watch it, Mister!"

The Bounty Hunter blinked out of his thoughts. His eyes widened and he pulled Warlock away from a child standing in the road. Huddled close was an old crone. Probably in her late seventies from what he could tell. Mostly covered in a black tattered hood.

"My apologies," the Bounty Hunter croaked, reminding himself he should take a drink of water. He pulled the cork of his waterskin and knocked back a soothing drink of spring water. There wasn't much left, by the weight of it. The whiskey was playing with his mind. A dopey, dreamy, sense of floating.

The liquor hit him harder than he thought it would.

"Ya almost killed this baby," the crone wailed as he passed. "Damn drunk is what ya are! Can smell it comin' off ya!"

The Bounty Hunter shook his head and nudged Warlock into a light gallop. The woman's shrill voice cut through the alcohol fuzz clouding and bashed his brain like steel hammers. Even with her shrieks fading, those hammers kept on knocking. Pain pulsed through his head and the world spun around him. Trapped, he couldn't get out of the spinning. Translucent waves riddled the air—

He leaned over the side of the horse and vomited onto a cactus.

Now he remembered why he didn't drink very often. His gut couldn't handle the liquor. Either that, or he didn't have a tolerance for it. Most likely both.

The Bounty Hunter wiped his mouth with the back of his hand and squinted at the midday horizon. The sun, hidden behind a wall of clouds, gave the world he rode in an ethereal glow. Almost goblin skinned. Green, flecked with gold hued in red. The dry world around him would no doubt burn at any given second. A simple cigar could ignite an inferno. Bright orange rays of sunlight shot out through holes in the clouds, as if God himself was trying to break free of the fluffy prison.

All this was in a single gap of clarity, then his vision blurred over again.

Yes, he was drunk, and it took all his strength and will to sit upright in the saddle. He tugged on the reins to slow Warlock down a bit. He could no longer hear the cries of the old crone. He should stop and sleep it off. Find a cold creek and dunk himself. Anything to get all the fuzziness out of his head.

Instead, he leaned forward, face in the gentle whisper of Warlock's mane. He breathed in the dusty scent of travels and—

6

"Is he hurt?"

A groan rolled out of the Bounty Hunter. Something tickled his nose and he sneezed. Hair? Why was there hair in his nose? What...

"Git'im off'in that ol'stang'n git'im inside," a woman shouted. Nothing like the old crone. This was a woman in her prime. A woman with no man to guide her. A woman of herself.

A rarity, indeed.

Even so, the Bounty Hunter remained in darkness. He couldn't feel or see. Only hear.

"Wren! Where ya at? Fetch some water'n'a rag. Ben, lay'im on your bed."

"But, Mama," a younger voice said, maybe a girl. "What if he's a bad man?"

"We'll see 'bout that later. Go on now'n'git that water."

The Bounty Hunter drifted back into the deep darkness. One with no sound. No feeling.

A vast space of...nothing...

***

The Bounty Hunter woke to the chirp of crickets and smell of fresh baked bread. He squinted in the darkness he found himself draped in.

Nearby, small snores tangled with the symphony of crickets. It all created a strange, but soothing stew for the ears. He sat up and felt for his guns. Gone. They took his guns, whoever they were. A spike of dread plunged into his stomach. If he took his guns off, they were never very far. He carried them as much as possible, even sleeping. This world had teeth and claws and was rampant with viciousness. The only things a man could trust were his guns. Lifelines in a world chomping at the bit to kill you.

He drew in a breath and blew it out slowly, attempting to quell his nerves.

The small snores never paused, nor did the crickets stutter.

The space around him was like the cool resonance of autumn. A chill kissed his cheeks like back in Iowa, telling him winter was on its way. A shiver scuttled under his skin like hundreds of tiny, black spiders.

Yeah, he couldn't stay here. Something in his gut told him he wasn't safe.

The Bounty Hunter stood and waited for his head to ease and not be so swimmy. They left his boots on, and the floor under him felt like wood. The planks would creak. The hard heels of his boots would clunk. If he was going to sneak out of this place the boots needed to go. He went about doing just that when raspy humming found his ears.

He straightened and frowned. His gaze drifted through the thick darkness of the room he stood in. At least, he reckoned it was a room. The humming grew louder for a moment or two, then faded to a whisper just as the Bounty Hunter's sight happened on a sliver of yellow light he hadn't noticed before. He stared at the sliver for a while, not sure how to proceed. But at least there was a direction out of the room. Well, he hoped so, anyway.

The Bounty Hunter moved toward the sliver of light, mindful of his step. The sliver of light widened as he approached. Growing to first an inch, then two...now three...

Through the crack of light in the darkness, he spotted what appeared to be a dinner table. Nothing fancy. Just a few wooden planks nailed to two by fours for legs. At least, that's what he could make out, anyway.

The scent of fresh bread filled his mouth with saliva. He swallowed and cringed when his throat made a dry click.

The humming stopped and the Bounty Hunter froze, heart stuttering.

Where the hell are my guns? He squinted through the narrow gap in the darkness. *Who are these people*?

On one hand, they probably saved his life. That whiskey hit him hard. Unless…it wasn't really whiskey. Poison, maybe? It wouldn't be the first time he'd been tricked when it came to booze. On the other hand, many folks who appeared sane on the surface were really bags full of crazy, deadly snakes.

He waited for as long as his nerves would allow and started forward again.

"Y'ain't gotta sneak, Mister."

He stopped walking, jaw clenched. It was the same strong woman's voice he'd heard before darkness took over. He was only about three feet from the gap in the darkness. The smell of bread was even stronger now.

"C'mon out," said the woman. "Ain't gonna bite ya." A thick chuckle followed. So thick, the Bounty Hunter wondered if maybe there was a man in the next room too.

He sighed and his fingers caught the edge of a door. He slowly pulled it open to reveal a full kitchen and eating area not quite large enough to be considered a dining room. A rustic dining table stood directly in front of him. Two loaves of bread sat at the center of the table on tattered cloth. A bit off to the right was a sink and counter space. A few splintery cupboards with what appeared to be animal bone handles.

Beyond all that was a living area. Of course, there was the crackling fire in a large fireplace to the right. To the left, there appeared to be a lounge chair and other chairs, though most were blanketed in darkness.

"Gotta keep the fire burnin' on a night like this," the woman said. "For the kids."

Oddly, he didn't spot her in a rocking chair until he stepped through the doorway.

"Close the door," the woman said. "Don'wan'em wakin' up yet. Too early."

The Bounty Hunter closed the door and faced the woman in the rocking chair once more. In the flickering firelight she appeared to be grinning. He saw a painting of a goblin once and that grin reminded the Bounty Hunter of it now. When she rocked back, her entire head disappeared into the shadows. A headless woman.

Or a headless goblin.

"Well, c'mon, boy," the woman croaked. "Time we palaver."

The Bounty Hunter's gaze drifted over every surface in search of his guns. No sight of them.

Shit.

He walked as quietly as he could across the kitchen and dining area, boots clunking despite this, and into what appeared to be some kind of sitting room. The only light was that cast by the fireplace in the kitchen. He stepped aside so he could see her better and light up the room a bit.

This close, though, he noted she wasn't grinning, but merely smiling. A warm, grandmotherly smile. Her eyes sparkled like diamonds in their sockets. She wasn't old, but getting up there, he supposed. Maybe late fifties. She was a considerably large woman with broad shoulders and strong arms, but that's all he could really determine while she rocked back and forth.

The rocking chair creaked under her. "Was quite drunk when we found ya."

The Bounty Hunter nodded. "I reckon so. Thank you for mending me."

The woman waved and huffed. "Only Christian thing t'do, boy." She stopped rocking and looked him up and down. "Y'a Christian, ain't ya?"

The Bounty Hunter nodded.

The woman returned the nod and she puffed her cheeks out in a sigh. She eyed him. "Thought so. Ya got the drink in ya, though. Drunk as a skunk when we found ya." She paused, frowning. "Might not be jus' booze though. Word is someone's been goin' round poisonin' whiskey barrels."

As farfetched as it sounded, the Bounty Hunter agreed. There was more than just the liquor that got to him. He was most definitely poisoned and would have died if not for...

"What's your name?"

The woman chuckled. "They call me Aunt Winnie. Run a sorta boardin' like house here, for wayward children." She cocked her head. "And you?"

The Bounty Hunter was tempted to tell her his real name. Even closer than he'd been with Coy for some reason. Still, he stowed the urge and said, "I have no name."

Aunt Winnie stopped rocking and squinted at him. It was still difficult to make out all the features of her face, but the movements gave certain gestures away. The wrinkling of the forehead. The upward scrunch of her cheeks. Her hands slowly gripped the chair's arms until the wood creaked.

"Ya ain't got a name?"

The Bounty Hunter shook his head and frowned. Her chest was heaving now, as though she was at a loss for breath. He took a few paces back and wished he had never bothered with that old saloon. None of this would be happening.

Where are my guns? He spared a glance around, but the darkness of the room was too much.

"Ain't no one ain't gotta name," Aunt Winnie said. Her voice took on an odd gravelly tone. She still squinted at him.

The fire in the kitchen crackled and, for a moment, that was the only sound.

"Call me Bounty Hunter," he said.

Winnie blew out a long breath. Too long to be a sigh. Something of exasperation, perhaps. He wasn't so sure.

"'Slinger, are ya?"

To this, the Bounty Hunter did not reply. There was no need and he let it float in the air a moment before he said, "Where are my guns?"

Winnie cocked her head to the side. As though she was curious. "What do ya need 'em for?"

"I thank you for your hospitality and good graces, but I have business farther north and need to set out."

Her hands gripped the arms of the rocking chair again and quaked. The wood cried out with the strain.

The Bounty Hunter took two more steps backward.

"Ya 'bout died," Winnie spat. "I saved ya. I nursed ya..." She rose out of the rocking chair like some dark creature from Hell itself. A woman of mass. Of muscle and will. "I never said ya could leave."

"Listen," the Bounty Hunter said, "I have no quarrel. I was thanking you."

"S'pose ya are tellin' the truth. You're welcome. But..." Winnie stepped fully into the firelight.

The Bounty Hunter's heart thudded against his ribs. The woman's face was a disfigured mess of scars. Her eyes were two twinkling black orbs set in twisted, pink flesh.

"A man with no name," Winnie continued, "is a man who can't be trusted. He can't be let t'live."

The Bounty Hunter moved to punch her but massive arms like slabs of granite wrapped around him. Hot breath buffeted the top of his head. The more the Bounty

Hunter struggled, the more those massive arms squeezed. The beast holding him grunted.

Winnie, in all her scarred and twisted appearance, grinned at him.

A goblin's grin…

Hungry. Predatory, like those shiny black eyes.

Lifeless.

The smell of the beast holding him made him belch a bit of puke out onto the floor.

Aunt Winnie glanced at it then returned her attention to the Bounty Hunter. "Ya gotta weak stomach? Well…" She waved a hand at someone behind the Bounty Hunter. "I got some'in t'help ya with that."

A dull scraping noise vibrated from one wooden wall to the other before pummeling into the Bounty Hunter's ears. A sound like an axe being dragged across the floor. Something heavy and metallic.

The giant man holding the Bounty Hunter chuckled. His voice, so deep, it quaked the Bounty Hunter from the inside out.

The scraping noise grew louder and louder.

The Bounty Hunter, trying to quell his fear, sent a few sharp kicks back into the beast's legs.

A couple of grunts followed. The sound of steel scraping wood.

"We got places for men without names here," Aunt Winnie said, moving closer. So close he caught a whiff of her breath. Dead fish was the closest he could think of. "Here, men with no names are on the menu…"

The scraping stopped and Winnie stepped aside.

A thin young man with hollow cheeks and even hollower eyes, slouched in front of the Bounty Hunter. He was nude except for a twist of tattered and filthy cloth around his hips. His hair hung in thin, dark strings over parts of a ghoulish face.

"This here is Elroy," Winnie spouted from somewhere in the shadows. "M'youngest boy. He does all the choppin'."

Elroy snorted and grinned, revealing a mouth full of black, rotting teeth. There was the sound of metal scraping across wood and Elroy slowly moved a long scythe he had hidden behind to the forefront.

"Let'im go, Eddie," Winnie said. "Elroy's got'im."

The beast holding the Bounty Hunter grumbled but released him and moved away, leaving Elroy to his own devices.

The scrawny young man advanced, and the Bounty Hunter shifted his stance. He moved to the side while Elroy approached. His hands curled into tight fists.

"The matter?" Elroy hefted the scythe. "Scared of a lil'ol harvestin' tool?"

The Bounty Hunter's gaze narrowed on Elroy. The deadly focus of a gunslinger sizing up an enemy. He ignored Winnie's giggling and the beast's grunts somewhere behind him. All that mattered was Elroy and the harvesting scythe he wielded. The very thing the Grim Reaper himself used to harvest souls.

"Ya ain't gon'fight," Elroy said. His voice was airy and oddly soothing. "This'll be over soon, fella."

The Bounty Hunter remained perfectly still. So still, his heart slowed. His focus centered on Elroy. The crackling of the fire faded to conspiring whispers. The giggles from Winnie and the grunts from the beast man disappeared. It was only Elroy and him. Scrawny, wiry, Elroy with his deadly scythe. The Bounty Hunter released a slow breath through his nose.

The focus was necessary. The silence around him...a must.

It was in this focus, this silence, where he could hear the tendons in Elroy's arms creak when he began to swing the scythe. The slight inhale of breath. In the stillness, the very air shifted. A swirling motion. Pressure as air was rushed toward the Bounty Hunter by Elroy's attack.

If not for all of this, he might not have been able to gauge the young man's movements as well.

A lesson his mother taught him long ago. Focus. Listen. React.

Attack.

Elroy swung the scythe in a sharp arch. A move meant more to incapacitate, rather than kill. A swing to the legs.

The Bounty Hunter jumped back, moved to the side, and yanked the scythe from Elroy. The boy blinked. Absolutely dumbfounded. Clearly, no one had ever done that to him before. Everyone fell victim to the curved blade eventually.

Everyone.

A growl and a mountain of a man thundered toward him. So heavy, his footfalls shook the wooden floor.

"Get'im, Eddie," Winnie screeched from the shadows.

The Bounty Hunter swung the scythe in a full horizontal arc. The swing lopped Elroy's head off and the blade sank deep into Eddie's bare, grimy, barrel of a chest with a sharp thwack.

"Elroy," Winnie cried. "M'boy! *No*!

Blood sprayed from Elroy's stump as the body staggered, managed a couple of awkward steps and finally collapsed. The Bounty Hunter wiped splatters of blood from his face and turned to Eddie just as a massive hand closed around his neck.

With his huge frame blocking the firelight, the Bounty Hunter couldn't make out any features, or if Eddie was even really human at all.

"Kill'im," Winnie shrieked. "Kill'im! For y'brother!"

The hand around the Bounty Hunter's neck squeezed tighter and tighter. He kicked at the mountain of a beast.

He punched at it. He tried everything his frazzled mind could fix on. None of it worked.

Gray clouds rolled in as his struggles weakened. No longer could he draw in a breath. The world hazed over in a mess of blurriness. Every sound turned to mere, meaningless sighs. This was it, then. He couldn't best the beast man, Eddie. He couldn't outwit him now. All was chaos....

Chaos...

The Bounty Hunter blinked. Coy mentioned something about chaos. About people in general...

Images of Ana shuffled before his mind's eye. Images of his daughter, lost and dying if he didn't send more money...

Despite strangulation, the Bounty Hunter roared.

The hand around his neck loosened a bit.

Just enough.

He wrenched the hand off him, yanked the scythe out of the beast's chest and moved away before the howling man lunged for him.

"*Eddie*," Winnie shouted.

Eddie charged like an angry rhinoceros, and the Bounty Hunter swung the scythe. The beast moved, however, and instead of cutting Eddie's head off, the blade sank into the side of his head.

Eddie grunted and veered away, crashing into Winnie's rocking chair. He dropped to his knees, whining as he tried to pull the blade out of his head.

"You sonofabtich," Winnie said. The last was all in one word.

The Bounty Hunter turned just as she ran wailing out of the shadows holding a large knife above her head. A scarred banshee fueled by sorrow, rage, and utter madness. He pivoted, let her stumble by, and slammed a fist into the back of her head hard enough to drive her to the floor.

Eddie, having given up trying to pry the scythe blade out of his skull, simply laid there sobbing.

The Bounty Hunter thought he heard the giant man mumble something like, "Sorry, Mama. I dyin'."

Winnie growled and lifted herself off the floor. The Bounty Hunter kept his distance.

The knife was no longer in her hand, though, but buried in her chest. She fell on it when he punched her. She made a few gasping breaths and shuffled toward him, hand outstretched. Blood dribbled down the corner of her twisted mouth. Her dark eyes glimmered in the flickering firelight. Her breaths turned wheezy, her movements sluggish. A thin whine built in her throat.

She approached and the Bounty Hunter retreated.

"M-Mama?"

Winnie's dark eyes widened. Her gaze shot to the right of the Bounty Hunter and her face rippled in sorrow. The whining in her throat began as choked sobs. Her mouth worked to form words, but nothing other than weak cries came out.

To the Bounty Hunter's right stood a young boy, maybe six, rubbing sleep seeds from his eyes. His dirty blond hair was a corkscrewed rat's nest on his head. Grime streaked his cheeks. He wore a tattered set of pajamas. In the crook of one arm, he held a stuffed bear that was missing both eyes and the stuffing poked out from a split seam in its neck.

Winnie collapsed to her knees. Her outstretched hand moved from the Bounty Hunter to the boy.

"Mama? Why ya bleedin?"

The Bounty Hunter's heart stuttered. And ache spread throughout his chest.

Despite the madness running rampant through the family, there was also love. A mother's love for her children.

And the Bounty Hunter just took that away.

Never mind that they planned on killing and eating him. Just never mind that at all…

Winnie managed a whisper. Only one word.

"Baby."

She then fell forward, face first onto the splintered floor.

"Mama?" the boy said, cautiously moving toward her. "Mama, are ya—"

The Bounty Hunter swooped the child up into his arms and carried him outside. He placed the boy down, told him to stay put, and ran back into the cabin.

Winnie was dead. So was Eddie.

The Bounty Hunter sighed and wished there could have been another way, but alas…

He rummaged through every cupboard and drawer, every room, for his guns. He found bags of what appeared to be jerky (probably not beef or hog, either) and other miscellaneous household things. But no guns. No hat, either.

The only room he hadn't searched was the one he woke up in. He moved the loaf of bread and upturned the table. He broke off a leg, wrapped some old cloth he found near a rusty sink around it and lit it from the fire in the fireplace. The torch wouldn't last long, but it would serve to see for a minute or so.

Upon stepping into the room, he noted a lumpy straw mattress and pillows, a heavy, filthy quilt. The place where the kid and the Bounty Hunter slept. Odd. Why would Winnie put him, a stranger next to her sleeping son?

He moved on, swept the torch slowly back and forth until he came to a closet with a canted door. He tried pulling it open, but it was stuck. Not locked. The knob still turned in all its squeaky annoyance. The Bounty Hunter gave the door a hard yank and it rattled open. The hinges squawked while he dragged the door over the floor. So badly tilted, the corner of the door dug into the wooden planks. The result was more work than there needed to be.

He stepped back and shined the light of the sputtering torch into the darkness of the closet.

The Bounty Hunter gasped and stumbled back a few paces, heart whip cracking. Neatly stacked was a wall about five feet high of human skulls. Each of them appeared clean and flawlessly intact.

A shiver passed through the Bounty Hunter.

Then his gaze happened on the worn leather of his gun belt and holsters. His hat rested on top.

The torch sputtered, threatening to go out. Most of the cloth had burned away. He grabbed the belt, tossed the torch onto the straw bed without thinking, and secured his guns. Both appeared undamaged. He snugged his hat on and—

He only heard the roar a second before Eddie crashed into him with enough force to drive him into the log wall. Pain exploded through his back and no matter how hard he tried to stay standing, his legs buckled.

Towering over him, Eddie's breathing reminded him of bubbling stew. How the big man hadn't died was beyond the Bounty Hunter.

"You," Eddie managed through a fit of gurgles. "Mama…"

Eddie lunged.

The Bounty Hunter drew his right revolver and sent four bullets into the beast's forehead. Hot blood splattered the Bounty Hunter's face. Eddie gurgled, and toppled forward. His head struck the wall directly above the Bounty Hunter.

Moving quickly, the Bounty Hunter darted out from under Eddie before the big man collapsed.

It wasn't until then he noted the room was on fire. The straw bed, the entire wall and spreading along the floor toward him. The wooden planks were so old and dry, it was like they were made of kerosene.

He ran out of the cabin as the fire raged on behind him.

He turned, watching the side with the room he woke up in engulfed in flames and…

"Mama! Mama, wake up!"

The Bounty Hunter's eyes widened. He glanced around, but the boy wasn't out there with him. He was—

"No." The Bounty Hunter sprinted for the burning cabin.

The front door wouldn't do. Flames already licked around the jamb and climbed up the door itself. A single window about fifteen feet to the left of the front door caught his eye. He sprinted to it and, using the butt of a revolver, broke the glass.

"Kid," he shouted.

"M-Mama…" The boy's voice was barely heard over the gathering flames.

"Over here, kid," the Bounty Hunter shouted. "Your house is on fire!" He stuck his arms through the window so he could pull the boy out quickly. "I'm over here! Follow my voice!"

The kid began coughing harshly and the Bounty Hunter's heart sank. "Over here, kid!"

A few coughs, and the boy said, "Mister? Can ya help my mama?" Coughs. "I think…I think she's sick."

The Bounty Hunter's heart sank even more.

"She's gone, kid," the Bounty Hunter said. "C'mon. Over here at the window. I'll keep you safe."

A series of coughing followed.

"I can't leave Mama. I can't!"

The Bounty Hunter, deciding the boy was too scared for anything, lifted himself through the broken window. The air, or lack thereof, choked out any breathing. The smoke was so thick it took him longer than he wanted to find the boy. The fire was already crawling through the kitchen.

The boy kneeled beside his dead mother. He was shaking her and telling her to wake up through coughing fits.

The Bounty Hunter swept the boy up and jumped through the window before the fire engulfed the rest of the cabin. The kid screamed. He kicked and tried to gouge out the Bounty Hunter's eyes. The Bounty Hunter ran away from the burning cabin to a nearby shed.

He burst through the door and a large, black horse neighed. The boy screamed, thrashed and punched him in the face. A terrified, traumatized child. A young boy who had just lost his entire family, no matter how grotesque they were. To him, they were family and he loved them.

The Bounty Hunter did what he had to. He found a length of rope and tied the boy's wrists and ankles together. He then hoisted the wailing boy onto Warlock and tied him to the saddle. Not something he wanted to do, but he needed to get the kid away from everything. The boy needed time to calm down. Probably not the best way for a child, he reckoned, but it was a must for now.

He gave Warlock a gentle kick and the horse galloped out of the old shed. The cabin was an inferno and whatever lived there lived no more. The Bounty Hunter made sure the boy didn't see the blaze and turned Warlock southwest. Not the direction he wanted to go, but it would, despite the heat, save the kid from seeing his family home on fire.

The Bounty Hunter gave Warlock an extra nudge and all three raced into the night.

7

Dawn kissed the sky with reds, pinks and yellows. Soon the sun would peek above the rocky horizon and scorch the earth once more.

The boy hadn't spoken, or sobbed for that matter, since they fled the burning cabin. And with a few stops along the way, he barely drank any water. The skin around his eyes was swollen and red from crying so much. Dried snot caked his spot between his nose and upper lip. The rest of the boy's face was slathered in dirt and God knew what else and he stank to high Heaven.

So, when they came to a nice green patch with a small creek, the Bounty Hunter untied the boy.

The boy frowned, as though he didn't understand.

The Bounty Hunter smiled and pointed at the bubbling creek. "Wash up. I'll get us somethin' to eat."

The boy glanced at the creek, then blinked at the Bounty Hunter. "I…I don'know how."

"Well," the Boutny Hunter said, "let's see what we can do then. C'mon."

He led the boy to the creek and kneeled. He cupped water in both of his hands and scrubbed his dusty face. The water was cool on his hot skin, sweet on his lips. With the second scoop of water, he scrubbed, showing the boy how to wash his face.

The boy, still frowning, kneeled beside the Bounty Hunter and cupped his hands. He dipped them into the sparkling stream and smiled. "Cold."

The Bounty Hunter chuckled. "Yes. But that's best to wake ya up in the mornin'. A good splash on the face is better than coffee sometimes."

The boy brought his hands out of the water, drew in a breath and splashed his grimy face. He gasped, wiped water from his eyes and splashed more water. And more.

He rubbed. He splashed. And before long, his face was that of a healthy boy. Without prompt, the boy jumped into the creek, and dunked his head. The stream flowing away turned murky. That was how dirty the boy was and the Bounty Hunter's heart ached.

The creek was a bit too deep to leave the boy alone, so the Bounty Hunter waited. When the boy figured he was clean enough, the Bounty Hunter started a large fire for the boy to dry by and went on the hunt for breakfast.

He was still aware that Sheriff Jones had men out there searching for him and, perhaps, a big fire wasn't the smartest thing to do, but the boy needed to dry off quickly and a fire was the best for that, besides wind, of course.

Wary, stomach grumbling, the Bounty Hunter stumbled upon a turkey nest with three large eggs. Shrill gobbling snapped his attention around to find the daddy bird charging at him full speed. Without thought, the Bounty Hunter drew a revolver and blew the daddy turkey's head clean off. He stepped away while the bird flopped around until it fell still.

Somewhere near, another gobble sounded. The Bounty Hunter gathered the eggs in his satchel and picked the dead turkey up. Mama turkey was still out there, and he thanked her for her sacrifice. Even if she didn't want it. Such was the way of survival. He didn't like it, but he also needed to live, and she would eventually find another mate and deliver more eggs. Nature being nature and healing itself in time, he reckoned.

At camp, he gutted and plucked the bird, not really sure how he would turn it into jerky for their travels. As for the eggs, he always carried a flat skillet in Warlock's saddle bags. Everything would stick because there was no lard, but he didn't care. They needed food. They needed to stay strong. Couldn't be helped and he would deal with the sticking when the time came.

The boy watched all this with mild curiosity scrawled over his face. Perhaps he hadn't seen someone cook a turkey? Perhaps. The Bounty Hunter supposed turkey wasn't a meal they served during family dinners anyway. Or beef. Or pork. The boy was young and witnessed much, but he hadn't been fully tainted yet. Six was an inquisitive age, the Bounty Hunter knew through his daughter Ana. It was also an age where real remembrance begins.

So, the Bounty Hunter made sure his movements were slow while he cooked their eggs and roasted the turkey over the fire. He watched while the boy poked at his plate of eggs for a moment or two, then took a tentative first bite. He watched the boy's face light up and heard the mmm sound escape the boy's throat. When the boy devoured the rest of the egg in seconds, he knew all would be well.

No, the boy hadn't been tainted too deeply, thank God.

They ate their eggs and while the turkey roasted on the makeshift spit over the fire, they leaned back against an old log.

"That was good," the boy said.

The Bounty Hunter nodded. "It was."

The boy frowned and shook his head. "What was it?"

"Eggs," the Bounty Hunter said and wished he had a cigar to smoke. He craved the taste of tobacco on his tongue.

"Eggs," the boy mused and smiled through the thin canopy of trees to a crisp, blue sky.

The Bounty Hunter nodded. "Soon as the turkey is done cookin' ya can give'er a try too."

"Turkey," the boy said, still staring at the sky.

The Bounty Hunter nodded. "What's your name, kid?"

"Michael." His smile lengthened. "Like the angel, Mama said."

Of course, the boy wouldn't forget his mother. No child, unless taken away before recognizable memories were stored away, would forget their own mother.

"Michael," the Bounty Hunter said. "A good name."

"Mama said I can save us," Michael whispered and rolled away. Sniffles soon followed. "Like the angel savin' people."

The Bounty Hunter didn't know what to say so let the issue drop for now. He wasn't much good at philosophies or analogies. He could console, though now didn't feel like the right time and while the turkey's skin crackled and browned, he knew what needed to be done.

8

What turkey they didn't eat, the Bounty Hunter stored in a pot, tied the lid down as tight as he could and placed it in the cool creek for overnight. It would keep it from spoiling, or so he hoped. The trick had worked more than once in his lifetime.

As they bedded down for the night, the Bounty Hunter gave the kid his bear skin blanket for the night and decided to keep watch.

He let the fire die down to winking coals.

If his hunters were still out there, and he was sure they were, he needed to be ready. If just one saw the smoke from the fire earlier, there was no doubt in the Bounty Hunter's mind they would be moving in. If they were already watching, they were no doubt waiting for him to sleep so the capture of kill would be easier. Boom. Boom. Both the Bounty Hunter and Michael dead.

So, he waited out the night wrapped in his wool blanket while Warlock chomped on some weeds nearby.

The Bounty Hunter sat against a tree and gazed at the utter darkness surrounding him. No stars. No moon. Just the dark and all the peculiar sounds stewing within.

***

Cold metal nudged his cheek.

The Bounty Hunter woke with a gasp, and went for his gun.

"Ah-ah," a soothing voice spoke from the shadows. "Put them hands up, boy."

And when the Bounty Hunter didn't move, the distinct click of a hammer being drawn back sounded.

"Ain't gonna ask ya again, boy."

The Bounty Hunter sighed and raised his arms. The fire was only dim coals now and he hated himself for falling asleep. He usually had quite a bit of control staying awake to keep watch. Did it many times and the one time that really mattered...he failed. Not only for himself but the boy.

Michael...

He moved to see if the boy was okay, but the man in the shadows said, "Shh, the boy is sleepin'. Best not wake'im."

The man's accent wasn't thick, so the Bounty Hunter assumed he must be from somewhere besides the Arizona Territory or New Mexico Territory. The Bounty Hunter kept his gaze in the direction of the man's voice. Waiting.

"Now," the man in the shadows said, "I want ya to stand up slowly. Go for a gun and I'll blow a hole in your head...then kill the kid. Ya play it right and we walk outta here just fine, both you and the kid'll live. Got me?"

The Bounty Hunter stood and nodded. How could the man see him in the dark? How...the coals. They gave off just enough light to see the Bounty Hunter and the boy, Michael. But the man in the shadows was just far enough away the light didn't touch him.

"Take them cannons off, boy." A rustling of weeds and there. A slight glint of light reflecting on glass. "Don't try anything either or I'll—"

The Bounty Hunter drew his right-hand revolver and fired with the speed all his own. The shot echoed throughout the small patch of trees. There came a light thump, followed by a gasping. The man in the shadows staggered out of the darkness toward the coals of the campfire. Sitting, wide-eyed, Michael cowered as the man with a hand on his chest shuffled closer.

The Bounty Hunter caught up, yanked the man away from the boy and shoved him to the ground. He rolled the man over.

"Jones?" the Bounty Hunter asked.

The man, one of the lenses of his glasses cracked and the wire frames skewed, coughed up blood and nodded.

The Bounty Hunter hunkered down beside the dying man. "How many more did he send after me?"

The man gurgled up more blood. His body trembled.

"How many?" the Bounty Hunter said.

"S-ix…" The man shook, spewed blood and released his final, bubbly breath.

"Wh-who is that?" Michael asked.

The Bounty Hunter stood. "A man just tryin' to make a livin'." He turned to the boy. "Get packed up. We need to leave."

Six, the Bounty Hunter thought.

He bested two, so there were four more out there hunting him.

They secured all the belongings to Warlock, even the turkey meat in the pot, doused the coals, and they set out embraced by the cool darkness of the night.

***

"Who is the boy?" Coy asked when they stepped into the cave.

"A good kid brought up in a bad home. Cannibals. Filthy."

Coy paused. "Cannibals?"

"People who eat people."

Coy frowned. "And this boy was born into it?"

"Yes."

Coy glanced around his cave and faced the Bounty Hunter. "I am too old to care for a boy so young."

"I'll come back when this is all over."

Coy sighed. "Okay. I will teach him what I can until then."

The Bounty Hunter smiled and placed a hand on Coy's shoulder. "Thank you, my friend. This is the safest place he can be."

Coy patted the Bounty Hunter's hand. "The boy will be here when you return."

"Thank you."

Coy gave a single nod and a smile.

Not long after, the Bounty Hunter hunkered down in front of Michael. The boy glanced over his shoulder. "Who's that?"

The Bounty Hunter sighed. "His name is Coy Wolf. He's gonna be takin' care of you for a while—"

"No," the boy said. Tears welled in his eyes. "I wanna stay with you!"

"Kid, look, I…"

Michael shot forward and wrapped his arms around the Bounty Hunter's neck and shoulders. A bear grip of an embrace.

In the Bounty Hunter's ears, Michael sniffled and said, "Please don't leave."

How strange, it was like the boy had already forgotten his family. Or, perhaps, came to a realization. They were his family, and he loved them, but came to the realization (as far as a six-year old can, anyway) that they might not have been very good people.

The Bounty Hunter sighed once more and hugged the boy back. "I will be back. Until then, Coy is a very nice man and will teach you many things."

Still, the boy refused to let go.

What do I do now? What—

"Do you know what this rock is?" Coy asked from behind the Bounty Hunter.

The boy sniffled, though didn't move or speak.

"It is flint."

The Bounty Hunter smiled.

It took the boy a few seconds, but, finally, his grip loosened. "F-Flint?"

"Yes. Want to see what it can do?"

Michael let go and stepped back. He wiped tears away from his cheeks. "Y-You'll be back? Promise?"

The Bounty Hunter smiled. "I promise."

Although, he wasn't so sure he'd make it back. And if he did, it wouldn't be for a while. Months. Maybe even years...

The boy gave him a quick hug, then ran to Coy and the cave without a single glance over his shoulder at the Bounty Hunter.

Just as well. He needed to get moving and cover his tracks here before nightfall anyway.

The Bounty Hunter gave the mouth of the cave a glance, then set out to find a new job.

For Ana.

9

He rode northwest again, though veered slightly more west than before.

California lands. Perhaps Upper Oregon. Didn't really matter so long as he could land a bounty job and set out right away. A larger town or city would be ideal and pay more. Santa Fe, or hell, maybe he'd travel further north anyway and check out Silverton up in Colorado. He needed to make up for his loss. Ana relied on him. Now more than ever.

His mind drifted from Ana to Michael. Back and forth for days which melded into weeks before he finally arrived at a town called Springwood. The name, heavily burned into a large plank above a tall archway, was his only greeting, however. The town wasn't small. Larger than most, except...

There appeared to be no life. No one rode around on horses. No coaches bringing travelers in or taking them out. No tinkling of a piano or harpsichord. No chatter of people. Only the breeze blowing sand into a mild dune over the road.

The Bounty Hunter frowned, though entered anyway. Maybe everyone was inside to avoid the blowing sand? That didn't make sense either, but he didn't have time to dawdle so pushed on. He paused, only once, in front of the town's grocery store. The widows were all bashed in. The sand had eroded much of the plank exteriors turning it into gray Swiss cheese.

Something dark and scrawny scurried from one side of the store to the other inside. The Bounty Hunter couldn't be sure if it was human or not. Didn't matter; he gave Warlock a gentle bump and hurried out of Springwood.

A ghost town, if ever there was one. One he never wished to visit again and fled quickly.

A day later he came to a living town, and much larger than Springwood, called Quartz Falls. The bustling of its people was almost overwhelming compared to the deadness of Springwood.

He found the Sheriff's Office and Jail, tied Warlock up next to the water trough, and went inside.

A single man, face sheened with sweat glowered at him from behind a rickety wooden desk. Bald on top, his scalp glimmered in the sunlight cast through the only window, barred, in the two-cell jail. One cell was a bit larger than the other. A small factoid the Bounty Hunter discovered through the years, the larger cells were typically for more than one drunk or another. The single cell was reserved for the worst.

Both were empty in Quartz Falls.

"Help ya, Mister?" the balding man behind the desk asked.

"Lookin' for work." The same line he had said throughout the years.

The man squinted at him. The Bounty Hunter noted the man's gaze slip to the guns just below his poncho. Finally, the older, sweaty man leaned back. His chair creaked with the strain. "Ain't no work here for ya."

"I'm a bounty hunter."

The man snorted. "That so? S'pose I'm the goddamn President, then? Got any papers showin' who ya are? You're in a place of law, ya know."

The Bounty Hunter rummaged in his satchel, brought out the same papers of identification he had always used and handed them to the sweaty man.

The man studied them for some time. So long, the Bounty Hunter wondered if he could read at all. Then he straightened and squinted at the Bounty Hunter again.

"Says 'ere ya got ninety-eight percent capture rate. What's the other two percent?"

The Bounty Hunter grinned. "Dead men."

The man blinked, folded the papers up and handed them back. "Never came across one like ya." He brought out a small box of slim cigars and offered the Bounty Hunter one. The man lit his cigar and blew silvery smoke. "I'm Sheriff Andrew Williams." He eyed the Bounty Hunter. "Ya don't have a name on your papers."

The Bounty Hunter plucked a wooden match from the Sheriff's desk and lit his cigar. He stared at the man through curling smoke. "That's right."

Sheriff Williams frowned. "Why?"

"No reason to know my name, I suppose."

"A man without a name is a man lost," Williams said.

The Bounty Hunter shrugged. "Maybe."

They smoked in silence for a time, then Williams leaned forward and pointed at something behind the Bounty Hunter. "If ya can get'em, you'll be a rich man."

The Bounty Hunter turned, finding a poster tacked to the wall of two men. One with a full mustache, the other with a bushy beard.

REWARD, the poster cried in big black letters at the top. Below, it read: THE RAMSY BROTHERS! $10,000 CASH REWARD ALIVE! $5,000 DEAD!!

Below all that, in smaller print: Alive or Dead, bring to Quartz Falls Sheriff Williams.

It wasn't the first time the Bounty Hunter had seen such a poster. Nor the first that duped him. Sometimes, even with the law, people were hard pressed to pay.

What stood out to him, however, was the stark white X scar on the right side of one of the brothers' forehead.

He drew on his cigar, blew out smoke and turned back to Sheriff Williams. "Where were they last seen?"

"Near the mountains. New Mexico way. A three-day ride from here, if memory serves right."

The Bounty Hunter nodded, turned, ripped the poster from the wall and approached the Sheriff. "I want half upfront and will bring at least one of the brothers in alive."

Williams chuckled. "I'll put'er in with the bank. Doubt they'll let that kind of money go. You're a stranger here. No one trusts a stranger."

"Right," the Bounty Hunter said. "I leave in the mornin'. Be sure to have it all set up before dawn." He tossed the poster onto the desk and walked out.

He found a nice stable to keep Warlock fed and watered and made way for the local hotel and saloon.

The Dripping Bucket, the sign proclaimed. Old, weathered gray, it was hard for the Bounty Hunter to make out the words. Splintered and swinging on rusty hooks a few feet above crooked batwing doors.

The plinking of the harpsichord and dreadful singing of some woman drifted out into the hot midday air. How they found the energy for all that, the Bounty Hunter would never know. He pushed his way through the squawk of the batwings and into The Dripping Bucket where he was assaulted by the barrage of rotten onions, cigar smoke, and beer.

The mingling of odors held him sway for a moment or two. Long enough to note the harpsichord player was shirtless, narrow chest glistening with sweat, and the singer, some lady in her late forties, perhaps, flouncing around in nothing but a stained bodice. Her hair was in salt and pepper disarray. Her freckled face was a sheen of sweat and grime. She sang some song in a voice like a fork scraping along a porcelain plate over and over. Cringeworthy.

Unlike the last saloon he visited, where he was poisoned, The Dripping Bucket was quite lively. And, despite the heat, the patrons were laughing and having a good old time. There appeared to be a poker game going at a large table in the back, barely lit by a single lamp. There were whores about, but this wasn't a brothel. They weren't waiting for men on the second-floor landing or calling out for someone to join them for a drink, on your dime, of course.

No, The Dripping Bucket was a fun place for cowboys and travelers to take a load off. Drink, eat, rest, and set out the next day. And, compared to the other saloon, this bar was long and polished to a high shine. The tender, a middle-aged man, maybe in his early forties, wiped every spot where a patron spilled booze or spit tobacco. He was a small, yet spry man with a shock of red hair and a smile which gleamed on his sweaty face.

No one took notice of the Bounty Hunter except for the tender as he approached the bar.

The redheaded tender nodded. "Help ya?"

"Bottle of whisk—" He caught himself, remembering last time. "Beer and a room for the night if ya got one."

"Mayhap I do," the tender said, smiling. So jovial. The man really loved his job, by the look. "Wanna room lookin' out over the river?"

The Bounty Hunter thought about it, then shook his head, preferring to keep distractions at a minimum. "Just a room, a bath, and beer."

The tender nodded and ducked under the bar. When he popped back up, he handed the Bounty Hunter a key attached to a blue poker chip with a small length of twine.

"Room six, sir. Be two dollars for the night."

The Bounty Hunter paid the man and went to his room. There, he bathed, ate a meal from the saloon's kitchen, and drank his fill of water. After, he chugged a couple of beers and called it a night.

The bed wasn't exactly luxury, nor like home, but it was one hundred times better than sleeping on the ground out in the cold desert night. It was what his sore, bruised body needed.

He didn't have much time to really contemplate much before darkness washed over him.

10

The morning brought with it a drunk whore on his floor and a man pissing out a window.

The Bounty Hunter slipped a revolver from the nearby holster and aimed it at the pissing man.

The man grunted. "First half is on the table." The man shook off, zipped up and faced the Bounty Hunter. "He expects one of the Ramsy brothers brought back alive or you don't get the rest of the reward."

"Not much of a deal if things go sour," the Bounty Hunter said, keeping his gun on the man.

The man, thin and tall, shirtless, shrugged. "It's the Sheriff's offer. I'm just the messenger." He dressed himself the rest of the way, buckled his gun belt and smiled at the woman passed out on the floor. "She's yours now. Have fun."

With that, the man left the room and the Bounty Hunter lowered the gun. He got out of bed, dressed, placed the woman on the bed and stuffed the cash into his satchel.

Outside, the birds were already calling in the morning.

***

The Bounty Hunter paid the stable master for housing Warlock and set out for the northeast.

The mountains…

11

He thought about his daughter, Ana, often. And Michael. He thought of Michael too and hoped all was okay with Coy.

Eventually, the mountains came into full view, growing larger and larger as he approached. The air had chilled a bit, though nothing drastic, but comfortable compared to the scorch-lands of the southwest. He had seen the mountains many times, of course, but they never ceased to impress. Torture to climb, just as bad trying to go around.

It was on his twelfth day, and about a mile from the base of the mountains when—

"Now!"

Eight men jumped out of the brush. All of them armed and pointing their guns at the Bounty Hunter. He yanked back on the reins, stopping Warlock. The horse gave a brief, surprised neigh.

A tall man with a thick, black beard stepped forward. "Give us your horse'n'ya live."

The Bounty Hunter's gaze narrowed on him for a second, then drifted to the man standing just a foot or two behind with an equally thick beard. They could have been the same person. And, without many deductions, he confirmed they were the Ramsy brothers by the stark white X scar on the right side of the man's forehead. The man who stood behind and off to the side. The one, the Bounty Hunter noted, with the deadest eyes of all.

A man approached Warlock's left side, younger than the Ramsy brothers, though missing most of his front teeth and wearing a brown hat with a limp, droopy brim, he had the appearance of an older man. He reached for the reins.

The Bounty Hunter drew his left revolver and pressed the muzzle against the man's grimy cheek.

"Don't," the Bounty Hunter said and shot a glare at the Ramsy brothers. "I'm just passin' through. I reckon, if ya wanna do this peacefully, you'll let me pass."

The Ramsy brother with the white X scar snorted. "Is that so?"

The Ramsy brother in front waggled his revolver at the toothless man held at gunpoint. "Kill'im and get it over with. You'll be dead before the bullet passes through his skull."

The Bounty Hunter eyed both Ramsy brothers, aware the other five men were closing in around him. They had him surrounded.

He grinned. Greater odds had been stacked against him than this.

The Ramsy brother with the X scar frowned at the Bounty Hunter. The one in front glanced back and forth at the closing circle of the gang.

"If ya want your men to live," the Bounty Hunter said, gaze fixed on the man with the scar, "call them off. Now."

"Or," said the Ramsy brother in front, "we kill you."

The Bounty Hunter bashed the man reaching for the reins across the face with his revolver, swung, fired a shot into one man's shoulder and was about to finish the other three off when someone boomed, "Enough!"

The Bounty Hunter faced the Ramsy brothers, ready to take them out.

The one with the X scar stepped in front of the other. "Who are you, stranger?"

"Just a man on his way east."

The brothers glanced at each other then back at the Bounty Hunter.

"Through the mountains?" the one with the scar asked.

"Why not around?" the other brother asked.

The Bounty Hunter shrugged. "Was hopin' for an easy pass through the mountains."

The brother without the scar chuckled. "Mister, ain't no such thing."

The Bounty Hunter nodded, playing his part as best as he could. "Heard there might be, so wanted to check. I'll go around, then." He tipped his hat at the brothers. "Much obliged."

He had Warlock turn a bit toward the south so he could—

"Stop," one of the Ramsy bothers said.

The Bounty Hunter could have kicked Warlock into a sprint, but knew if he did, they'd gun him and Warlock down. Like dogs or wolves, if he fled, they'd give chase and kill. So, instead, he faced the brothers once more.

The brother with the X scar gestured with his revolver for the Bounty Hunter to dismount. "It's late. Camp here with us for the night. We got food and water to spare if ya don't."

The Bounty Hunter frowned. Could it be a trick? Probably, it was. Still, he knew if he ran, they'd gun him down before Warlock made it more than a couple of strides. He didn't trust them, but there was no other choice either.

He nodded. "Maybe a good night's rest will do me well."

The man with the scar on his forehead smiled and gestured at his gang. "Put'em away, boys. This man is our guest for the night."

They did as they were told, though the Bounty Hunter noted neither brother holstered their guns until he dismounted and holstered his. Then, it was as though he was part of the gang. All the tension evaporated, and they all led him to their camp in a small clearing at the foot of the mountains.

They asked for his name dozens of times, though each time he declined, falling back on his old go-to: "Until we're pals, there's no reason for names. I won't ask for yours. You don't ask for mine."

The Ramsy brother with the X scar on the right of his sweaty forehead took his tan hat off and eyed the Bounty Hunter. His black hair was slicked back, shiny with grease in the light of the fire. "A man who can't give his name is a man with secrets."

The Bounty Hunter said, "Mayhap you're right."

The man he struck with his revolver, face dark with an oblong bruise and blood crusted around his nostrils, dropped a cloth sack onto the Bounty Hunter's lap.

"Jerky," the man said and sneered. "All ya deserve. If'n t'was up t'me ya'd be—"

"It's not up to you, Jinky," the Ramsy brother without the scar said. "Go see how Will is doin' an' tell Wendell t'bring some of that stew for our guest."

"But—"

"Now."

Jinky glowered at the Bounty Hunter for a second or two and stormed off.

Ramsy with the scar grunted. "Never mind ol' Jinky. He's harmless." He took a sip from a tin cup filled with water. They were all having water instead of beer or liquor. Water was more important, even to outlaws. He leaned back a bit against the boulder they made camp around. "Why ya need to get around the mountains?"

"Personal business." The Bounty Hunter tossed the jerky on the ground and made sure the Ramsy brothers saw him do it. He didn't trust anything they were willing to give him.

Neither brother seemed to care about the jerky.

"Not much for palaver, are ya?" the Ramsy brother without the scar said.

The Bounty Hunter shook his head. "Never have been, I reckon."

Night soon doused them in deep shadow, leaving only the light of the fire. As with the jerky, the Bounty Hunter didn't eat the stew. Wendell, an older, bald man, cross-eyed and a cluster of pimples festooned to one cheek, handed everyone a bowl. They all ate. Except for the Bounty Hunter.

No one seemed to care one way or another, save for Wendell.

"You don't like meat stew?"

The Bounty Hunter put on his best smile. "I'm not really hungry." A lie, he could eat an entire pig. But he didn't trust anyone in the gang. Not even the cook.

Wendell snorted and offered the Bounty Hunter's bowl to one of the Ramsy brothers. The one with the scar took it and dug in.

Not poison, then. But the Bounty Hunter didn't trust anyone, as a general rule. The only time his guard truly faltered was with Coy and the old saloon before The Dripping Bucket and Michael.

Once everyone was fed and some whiskey passed around, everyone bedded down for the night.

Three men were set out to watch.

The Bounty Hunter wasn't sure how far out they were into the woods. Lost track of them once they stepped out of the firelight.

He waited hours.

He waited until all he heard were snores.

Even so, he waited a bit longer.

The fire was nothing but red coals winking in the darkness when the Bounty Hunter rose and snuck out of camp. He would just have to come back for Warlock and hoped the Ramsy brothers wouldn't hurt the horse. That's all he had right now was hope.

In the morning, the brothers wouldn't know what hit them...

12

If the sun were a person, he would have shot it between the eyes for taking so damn long to usher in dawn. He sat on a large pine tree bow above the camp, wishing he'd grabbed the rifle from its case tied to Warlock. The range might have helped. Maybe not. Still, he felt more comfortable in an ambush situation with a good rifle at hand. Just in case there was a runner.

Gradually, the gang woke below him. Maybe sixty feet. The first to stir was Wendell, the cook. He sat up, lit a smoke, and got to work on breakfast. Which appeared to be oatmeal or grits, jerky, and coffee.

Eventually they gathered their bedding rolls and tied them to their horses. The only one left was the Bounty Hunter's and the only one who noticed his absence, at first, was Jinky. And only when a cord of wood rolled out from under the buckskin blanket, did the man sound the alarm.

"He tricked us! He's gone!"

Dropping their bowls of oatmeal or grits, the Ramsy brothers strode over to where the Bounty Hunter should have been sleeping. The Ramsy brother with the scar on his forehead yanked the buckskin off, revealing a bundle of their own firewood. He backed away a bit and shook his head.

"Fine'im. Don't kill'im, though. I'd like to talk to the bastard first."

For being the worst of outlaws, the Bounty Hunter thought they were pretty tame. Well, until the Ramsy brother with the scar drew his gun and blew roughly half of Jinky's head away in a spray of skull, blood and brains.

The entire gang froze, even the other Ramsy brother.

"Jinky was on watch detail," the man who the Bounty Hunter was beginning to think of as Scar, boomed. His voice crashed and bounced off every tree. He leveled his revolver on a big bull of a man. "Wayne. You were also on watch detail."

Wayne raised his arms. "We didn't hear'im."

Scar thumbed back the hammer of his revolver. "Sorry, Wayne."

"Wait," a voice, nearly a whisper from as high up as the Bounty Hunter sat.

Everyone turned and the Bounty Hunter followed their gaze.

A wiry man dressed all in black cloth. He crouched, fingers touching something in the dirt. "He went this way."

Great, the Bounty Hunter thought. *They have a tracker*.

Scar holstered his gun. "Pack up!"

The other brother caught Scar's arm before the man could get to his bedroll.

"Let'im. He's got nothin' on us. Don' know our names. Nothin'. Let'im be."

Scar yanked out of his brother's grip. "S'pose he's walkin through a town n'our wanted posters are everywhere? He tells the sheriff and they send out a bunch'o bounty hunters." Scar spat. "Bastard could lead 'em in our direction."

"We'd be long gone by then," Scar's brother said. "This is just wastin' time."

Scar took hold of his brother's shirt and yanked him in close. "Listen'n'listen good. No loose ends, remember?"

"Ya planned on killin'im this mornin', didn't ya?"

Scar shoved his brother away. "Yup. And why ya can't grasp that is beyond me. Lettin'im live..." Scar shook his head and dropped to a knee by his bedroll.

"They'd catch us b'fore we made it to that border." He sighed. "It'll be quick then we'll be on our way."

The brother nodded, and the Bounty Hunter took aim at his head. His aim, however, drifted to Scar's head. The real leader of the gang. The smartest and meanest. The head of the snake, so to speak. The Bounty Hunter drew in a breath, let it out, and squeezed the trig—

"Someone's in that tree!"

The shot intended to blow a hole in Scar's head merely kicked the hat off his head.

In a matter of seconds, they all knew where the Bounty Hunter was.

"Shit," the Bounty Hunter said and drew his other revolver.

Scar roared and pointed at the Bounty Hunter. "Shoot'im down!"

The Bounty Hunter sucked in a sharp breath and blasted Wendel in the head before he could pull the rifle from the scatterings of his cooking supplies. He flailed back in a mist of red. Before the man fell, the Bounty Hunter put a bullet into the man he already shot in shoulder. A man named Will. This time it was square in the chest. By the time he returned his attention to the brothers, they weren't in the clearing anymore.

The remaining two in the clearing were the big man, Wayne and a boy, maybe in his late teens. He wasn't sure what his name was but he sat on the ground tinkering with something the Bounty Hunter couldn't see. Neither tried to shoot at the Bounty Hunter.

A mild breeze kissed the Bounty Hunter's sweaty face while he searched for the Ramsy brothers and their tracker. He turned, mindful of his seating, but the brothers weren't behind him either. Like they'd disappeared. The Bounty Hunter clenched his jaw. His heart thudded heavily. He—

A shrill neighing sound, like a scream echoed throughout the woods and his heart stuttered.

Warlock.

"Good mornin', stranger with no name," Scar shouted. "How's the air up there?"

Another shrill neigh.

His breath caught in his throat like an old meat hook. He coughed, glanced around, but still couldn't spot the brothers or his horse.

"I'll give ya to the count of twenty to climb back down, or I'll chop the head off this beautiful horse."

The Bounty Hunter's lips tightened together. He shot the two in the clearing a glance. Both appeared to have forgotten all about him and were eating the remaining oatmeal, or whatever Wendel cooked up.

"Shit," he said and climbed down.

The moment his boots hit the ground someone was on him. Someone lightning quick and strong enough to bash him against the tree and take one of his guns before his brain had a chance to catch up. Cold steel pressed against his forehead and a man whispered, "Don't move."

Sharp clapping erupted. Not the swell of many people but the distinct loneliness of one.

"Bravo, stranger," Scar said, stepping out of some thick brush and hunkering down in front of the Bounty Hunter. "Ya almost had us." His smile drooped. "*Almost.* Ya really think the Ramsy brothers can be fooled so easily? Which sheriff sent ya?"

The Bounty Hunter's gaze focused strictly on Scar, though he didn't say anything.

Scar shoved the barrel of a six-shooter at the Bounty Hunter's mouth.

Before it made contact, the Bounty Hunter shifted away from the gun pressed against his forehead and punched the man who caught him, the tracker, in the twig and berries. The shift gave the Bounty Hunter enough room to draw his other revolver and shoot Scar's gun hand and roll away from the tracker who subdued him in the first place.

Scar howled in pain.

A shot cracked and trembled the air, but the Bounty Hunter didn't stop moving. If he did, they'd get him. So, he rolled, gained his feet and spun just in time to smack a black clad arm away. An arm with a hand holding a large, curved knife. A skinning knife, but longer. The tracker. The Bounty Hunter dodged a kick, but the man was quick and landed a fist an inch or so from his right ear.

The world winked out for a second. The entire right side of his head stung. He wheeled around trying to gather his bearings. Another fist struck his back. When everything came back together and the pain in his head wasn't so urgent, he caught a glimpse of the other Ramsy brother coming at him, right arm cocked and ready to deliver a hell of a blow.

The Bounty Hunter ducked, missing the fist, pointed the revolver, and fired.

The result was blowing most of the Ramsy brother's lower jaw off. Blood rained down on him and for a handful of seconds, everything stood still.

Gagging, the Ramsy brother dropped to his knees, eyes wide, clutching at the mess of his lower jaw. A whine made its way out of the bloody ruin of his mouth.

The tracker wrapped cloth around Scar's mutilated hand.

The Bounty Hunter scrambled to his feet, spun, and ran. He found Warlock behind a thicket, which was why he couldn't see the horse or the men torturing him. The torture amounted to a few cuts from what the Bounty Hunter could tell, and he'd later examine them better. He untied the reins, climbed on and kicked Warlock into a sprint away from the Ramsy brothers' camp.

Not south, but north. Still keeping close to the mountains for now. Their tracker would think it all easy.

Nevertheless, the Bounty Hunter's mind churned and a plan was born.

13

They would be taking care of Scar and burying the fallen Ramsy brother. Unless the man lived, which would be unfortunate without a lower jaw, but the Bounty Hunter had come to try and never underestimate his enemies.

For all he knew the bullet blasted right into the man's brain.

Regardless, all of that gave him a head start and enough time to create a bit of distance between.

Enough time to set a trap.

He had Warlock move into a drift of pine needles and quickly went about sweeping away the horse tracks as far back as one hundred feet and did the same with his own upon returning to Warlock. From then on, he stuck to the woods for a day, though didn't stray too far from the foot of the mountains. He didn't want to go around or pass through. His payday was somewhere behind him. Hopefully. If Scar decided not to pursue then the Bounty Hunter would have to double back and go after them.

Two days gone. If they went elsewhere, it would be several days more, turning what he figured, at first, as easy money into a nuisance.

On the second day, he veered back to the foot of the mountains where there was more of a path. He hoped the tracker was fooled for a bit. If not, the trap wouldn't work.

A small town came into view. Rare, so close to the mountains. He wasn't sure how far north he had travelled yet until his gaze happened on the town's sign.

WELCOME TO ROCKY MOUNT

SOUTHERNMOST POINT OF THE MONTANA TERRITORY

The Bounty Hunter blinked. *Farther north than I wanted. Oops.*

He sighed and nudged Warlock into town.

It was larger than it appeared from the rocky road, though still held an air of small and quaint. Perhaps it was because many of the homes and cabins were close together and only began to sprawl the more one ventured away from town. What also made it appear smaller was the town's square and main street, which did not have a name. The street itself was short, leading directly into the square where businesses flanked each other on all four sides. The buildings themselves were made of dark wood, which reminded him of walnut and stones.

Though carrying the air of small, the quaint part was rightly apt. And there was something else...

As he made his way up the main street, a strange energy tugged at the very marrow of his bones. It coiled in his gut like a cold snake. An odd energy he hadn't felt in other towns. People bustled like any thriving town, though, and no one really took much notice of him. Jolly plinking from a piano drifted through the air. The smell of roasted meat and onions caught his nose and his mouth filled with saliva. It had been days since he'd really eaten much of anything besides jerky and what he could hunt in such a short time.

People were laughing. Children playing.

Dominating the town square was a large fountain made of stones. Quartz. Granite. Limestone. So many others he couldn't recognize. A giant, beautiful display and judging by the flow of water from the top, it was built over a healthy spring. More than a few people sat around this either reading books and or talking to each other.

All in all, he had never come across a town so full of...life. Of laughter. The odd energy tugging at him dissipated and he realized it was only there because he wasn't used to such towns.

He needed to keep pushing north and away from the town, though took his time passing through. Which involved a side street to go around the square. He got to see more of Rocky Mount. The more he saw, the more he liked. The very essence of the place eased his nerves.

Hell, maybe someday he would call it home.

But days were a tricky thing. Only one could mean your last.

So, he continued north until a few miles out of town when he came across a cave leading into the mountains.

He stopped, dismounted Warlock and inspected the cave.

After a few minutes he stepped out and nodded. "Let's get to work, then."

He let Warlock graze while setting the trap he hoped would bring him the money he needed to send to his beautiful Ana.

The Bounty Hunter began digging a hole with the small shovel from his supply pack tied to Warlock. He smiled, thinking about his dear Ana.

She would be ten now, though last he saw her was on her sixth birthday. A day which would forever be one of his greatest memories.

He scooped dirt. The hole was about two feet deep. He kept digging and let most of the memory unfold for what he worried would be the last time.

August Tenth. The day was hot and the Bounty Hunter took Ana to the streams to play and cool down. He joined, of course. Splashing and laughing while the Iowa sun beat down on him. Later, he would have burns from the sun, but in the moment, he didn't care. Once all the splashing was done, little Ana decided they needed to catch crawdads. So, he took them to a nice calm spot in the stream where they did just that. Twenty in all. The

Bounty Hunter let one clamp down on his nose with one of its pincers. It hurt a bit while it dangled there, but Ana's laughter was worth it.

Once they were cooled down enough, the Bounty Hunter laid out a blanket so they could have a nice picnic. Ham sandwiches and potato salad. Ana's favorite. The cake would be waiting for them when they got home.

While they ate, the birds sang in the trees and the frogs belched from the weeds and the fresh streams bubbled. A breeze whispered through the trees, a lovely sigh to a day coming to an end as the sun lowered in the horizon. Crickets chirped as the Bounty Hunter gathered up all the left-over food and blanket from the picnic and led them back home.

Home was a cabin he built on wooded land near the streams. The prairies got too hot in the summer. Too dry. The woods were just fine with him. Better hunting too.

About halfway to the cabin, Ana wanted to be carried. Her little body was too tired from all the activities. She plucked at his whiskers and told him he needed to shave. She said she had to be Mommy since Mommy got sick.

Some memories brought on others by default. Images shuffled from Ana to Grace, his wife. Grace. He could still feel the warm tenderness of her lips. The way her smile lit up his soul, even on the darkest days.

Digging and digging, now, the Bounty Hunter shook off the tears. He needed to focus on setting the traps, but...

At the cabin, he brought the cake up from the cool cellar and placed a fresh candle in the center. He lit it and sang happy birthday to Ana until it was time for her to make a wish and blow out the candle. She clung to him while he cut the cake and served her the first slice. She was a princess, that day. And forever his princess she'd always be.

A shrill sound echoing from the mouth of the cave pulled him out of his memories and back to the present. He stood in a hole as deep as his thighs. Still not deep enough, but what was…

The sound came again. A long, shrill scream. Not human, as far as he could tell, though. His first thought was a mountain lion. He climbed out of the hole and drew a revolver. The scream came again, though little more than a mild echo through the cave's opening this time. Barely more than a whimper.

Still, the Bounty Hunter slowly entered the cave. It was too dark to see much so he backed out and made a note to get a fire going and set up a couple of torches. If there was something deeper inside the cave, maybe the light would draw it out more. For all he knew it was a mountain lion or raccoon lost in a tunnel. Even though both could see in the dark, perhaps the light would help in some way. Also, he'd rather be able to see it and be ready to shoot if need be.

There were still a few hours of daylight left so he continued digging and making his traps.

By the time he was finished, dusk had already settled in.

14

If they came tonight, it would be because of the fire.

The Bounty Hunter purposely set it ablaze outside of the cave. He then stuck a few torches between cracks and rocks inside the cave, which did, indeed, reveal a tunnel in the far back.

The fire itself was at the center of his traps, his bedroll stuffed with leaves to make it appear like he was sleeping outside. Instead, he planned on spending the night in the cave wrapped in a thick quilt his mom made so many years ago. He kept close to the mouth of the cave, while glancing at the tunnel just in case an animal emerged.

The sounds didn't happen again, though, so he largely forgot about the tunnel and focused on the crickets outside.

It was mid-summer and in Iowa, the corn would be up to his thighs. The cicadas would rasp throughout the day. Watermelons would be about ripe for harvesting out of the garden. Mosquitos would, no doubt, be a constant irritation. The long summer evenings sitting out on the porch with a beer or lemonade, the day's heat subsiding, though never really going away. The sweat trickling down the small of your back...

A loud snap and a cry of either pain or surprise, or both, blasted the night air, yanking him out of remembrance. He crept closer to the mouth of the cave.

"Ah, Hell." And the Bounty Hunter instantly recognized the voice.

Scar.

"Bastard set a trap! Git'im outta that pit. Careful!"

A moment later, a voice he didn't recognize said, "Got stabbed by stakes. He's bleedin' out."

Another snap and crash. A scream followed.

"Wayne," Scar shouted.

"Don't move," the voice he didn't recognize said. Smooth and calculating. "He set pitfalls all around the fire."

The Bounty Hunter shrugged off the quilt and drew both revolvers. His rifle was strapped to his back in a makeshift holster.

"How's Apple?"

"Hurt, but I stopped the bleeding," the unknown voice said.

"Wayne?"

"Hurt bad," Wayne muttered. "C-Can't get out."

"Bobby," Scar said. "Help Wayne out. Careful of that bedroll. Might be another trap."

The Bounty Hunter's heart thrummed. If his calculations were correct, there were only two men still capable of putting up a fight. The only problem was they were the best two out of the group. Bobby, the Bounty Hunter assumed, was the tracker. Not just a tracker, but someone who knew how to fight and fight well. Even without a weapon, he about subdued the Bounty Hunter.

Another cry of pain and...

"Got'im out," Bobby said. "Looks like...Wayne, hold still now."

Wayne howled and the Bounty Hunter imagined the big man rolling around in the fallen pine needles blanketing the ground.

"Got'im through the gut," Bobby said. His tone dropped a bit. "Not good."

"H-Help me," Wayne said. His deep voice had been reduced to a trembling whimper.

"Sorry, my friend," Scar said.

"Wha—"

A gunshot cracked the air.

"We'll bury him when this is over," Scar said and in a louder tone, "Come on out, stranger. That bag of leaves ain't foolin' nobody. Come on out n'I might show ya some mercy."

The Bounty Hunter backed away from the mouth of the cave, fingertips on the triggers of his guns. If Scar thought the mention of mercy would draw the Bounty Hunter out, the man wasn't as smart as he thought.

"Git Apple away from them holes, Bobby. Git ready."

The Bounty Hunter glanced around. He needed some form of protection when the bullets began to fly. A small boulder. Anything. Of course, he hadn't thought about a barricade. So much for careful planning.

Of course, he hadn't expected them tonight either. He figured he had a day or two to get everything set up.

"C'mon, stranger," Scar shouted. "Don't be shy."

A shaky young man's voice drifted into the cave, "J-Just l-light it and throw."

The Bounty Hunter frowned. What was the boy talking about?

"Apple is gone," Bobby said in a voice so low, the Bounty Hunter barely heard it.

"Fuck," Scar said. A long pause, then, "I'm gonna count t'three. If ya don't come out, we're comin' in."

It was supposed to be a threat but there seemed to be no real conviction in his voice. Nothing which conveyed an actual threat.

Maybe Scar was already giving up. He'd lost his brother and all but one man in their gang. When was enough...enough? Better to cut their losses and let it go. Not that the Bounty Hunter wanted that, but if he was in Scar's boots...maybe.

"One," Scar boomed.

The Bounty Hunter backed away from the mouth of the cave. The torches fluttered with the movement of air. One appeared to be on the verge of burning out. Not what he needed right now.

"Two."

The Bounty Hunter inched back toward the tunnel. If there was an animal of some sort in there, he would have to deal with it when the time came. Right now, though, what mattered was getting a good sightline on the opening of the cave. A good position for various attacks. Regardless if they came in guns blazing or tried to sneak in…he needed a good vantage point they wouldn't expect at first. But—

"Three."

His gaze fixed on the cave's opening. A space of four feet wide by at least ten tall. His grip on the butts of his guns tightened. He drew a slow breath in through his nose and out his mouth. A bead of sweat trickled down the side of his face, even though the night was quite cool.

He waited.

When nothing happened for a long space of time, the Bounty Hunter frowned. He straightened and moved toward the opening of the cave and—

A large ball flew through the opening so fast he barely had time to duck. The ball struck the rocky floor of the cave behind him with a flat thump. He spun in time to watch it bounce into the tunnel and disappear. A second or two later, he noted a strange hissing sound. A snake? No. It crackled too.

Crackled and hissed like a—

"Bomb," the Bounty Hunter said and ran for the opening.

Boom.

A force like ten men shoved him forward into a wall near the cave's opening, cracking his head on the stones. The noise of falling rocks was the last thing he knew before everything went dark.

15

An unknown space of time went by before the Bounty Hunter rolled over onto his back. Pain squeezed his head like an iron vise. Small rocks and dirt spilled off him with the movement. He coughed, trying to shove the pain back enough to open his eyes. The air was dry and full of grit. So much so that he—

"What's that?"

Scar? It sounded like Scar.

"I…I don't know. Never seen plants like that before."

"He's in there, I bet," Scar said.

"I don't—"

"C'mon, Bobby. Let's kill'im and get this over with."

The Bounty Hunter rolled onto his side just in time to watch the two men duck into a hole just inside the opening of the tunnel.

He coughed some more and sat up. Besides the constant thrum in his head, everything else hurt too. Even his toes. A groan escaped him while he tried to stand and failed. He tried again and leaned against the ragged stone wall of the cave, staring at the bit of light where Scar and Bobby had disappeared.

The Bounty Hunter staggered out of the cave and found Warlock. He should leave. Just get on the horse and ride away. There would be other jobs to make money from. Let Scar and Bobby face whatever fate awaited them. Just…go…

Instead, he stroked Warlock's thick mane and pulled the rifle from its holster on his back. He loaded up with as many bullets as he could pocket and fit in his belts.

"I'll be back, ol' pal," the Bounty Hunter told Warlock and stroked the spot between the horse's eyes. Warlock loved that when he could get it, the Bounty

Hunter knew. "But if I don't come back…just run. Be free."

Taking off the horse's saddle, he didn't know if Warlock understood that or not, though he hoped, in some way, the horse did. Warlock didn't ask for any of this and he should be free.

With that, the Bounty Hunter made his way back into the cave, picked his hat up, snugged it onto his aching head, and ventured to spot just beyond the start of the tunnel.

Peculiar reddish yellow light drew his attention to the right and…

There he stopped.

Stopped cold.

The Bounty Hunter blinked, rubbed his eyes and looked again. It was the same. His knees threatened to buckle. He caught himself from falling and gaped into a lost world.

All the green struck him first and the hardest. The thick brush and giant trees billowing with varying shades of green. The tall grass fields to the left. He looked away, trying to break free of it all. Trying to tell himself it wasn't real. Couldn't be real. And yet…

And yet…

Opening his eyes to gaze upon this lost world he noted how vast it appeared. How, even though in what should have been a massive cavern, it seemed to stretch on forever in every direction. Heat, humid and cloying, spilled out through the hole and engulfed him. He shivered at the change in temperature. Different smells touched his nose and fluttered away. Of green leaves and rich pine. Of lake water and something he could only think of as a lizard or frog. A lizard smell mingled with the dankness of a swamp frog. But that wasn't the last of the aromas flirting with his nostrils.

Stenches which lingered below the rest. Of sulfur...and rot. Something like a freshly struck match and a broken rotten egg vying for one's attention.

And, somewhere near, something shrieked. A lot like the sound he heard coming from the tunnel. It had indeed been an animal, though nothing like he ever knew. Not a mountain lion, or bear. Not a raccoon or anything native to the lands he traveled.

Something else...

The Bounty Hunter sighed, glanced around, and climbed into a lost world under the mountains.

The real badlands...

16

He slid down a rocky slope into a swamp.

The ground under his boots was mushy and squelched with every step.

The heat alone struck him first. Hotter than the southern border, yet so humid. Nonetheless, it was hard for him to breathe until his lungs got a bit used to the drastic change.

He had only been in the tropics once and hated every damn minute of it. This place…this lost world, these badlands, was like the southern tropics, only worse. So thick, the air was. So…strange…

He leaped from the swampy bit of land he set foot on and into a thick patch of weeds to the left, which proved to be solid ground. The Bounty Hunter walked away from the swamp and gave his surroundings a quick onceover.

What baffled him more than anything was…

"Where's the light comin' from?"

Indeed, if this world was under the mountains, how did the sun get in and how could it be as light as midday while it was night on the outside? The sky. Or whatever served as the sky, revealed nothing more than vast emptiness as far as his eye could see. Seemed the light source didn't reach that far up.

Which gave him more pause.

If the light only radiated so far upward, wouldn't that mean the source came from the ground? And, if so, what could be so powerful to create such an abundance of light?

The Bounty Hunter shook it off for now. He needed to find Scar and Bobby. The sooner the better too. He didn't like this lost world under the mountains. Every nerve hummed as he made his way out of the swamp and weeds to a clearing with a small creek trickling through it. No more than three feet at its widest and—

Something on the other side, just beyond the thick brush, chittering.

Heart stuttering, his grip on the rifle tightened.

The brush trembled and the Bounty Hunter took aim.

But what emerged wasn't what he expected. An old, fat raccoon, of all critters. It rose up on its hind legs and mewled at him, then dipped back down and lapped up some water. It fished in the shallow stream until it came up with a crawfish.

The Bounty Hunter released a breath he didn't realize he'd been holding and chuckled. He lowered the rifle and shook his head and tried to will his heart to stop pounding. He needed to relax a bit. There was no evidence of anything living in this lost world other than what he already knew. To assume anything would be—

It burst out of the bushes, latched onto the raccoon with a curved tooth mouth, and leapt back into the brush.

The raccoon never made a sound.

Backing away from the stream, eyes wide, heart whip-cracking against his ribs, the Bounty Hunter lifted the rifle and pointed it at the thick brush where the creature disappeared. If he didn't know any better, he'd think it was a di—

It scrambled out of the brush at him with a speed he only witnessed with a snake strike. It was about the size of two male turkeys stacked on top of each other. About as tall as him, at six feet or so. It ran at him so fast he didn't even have time to fire a shot before the thing plowed into him. Something sharp dug into his shoulders.

The Bounty Hunter roared in pain, tried to kick the creature off, though to no avail. Its claws were dug in. Not life threatening deep, but enough to hook him like a fish. Enough to control him with its strength. Which was more than a mere man. It hissed in his face, blowing the stench of decay and coppery blood into his face. Hundreds of curved teeth flashed and it took everything the Bounty Hunter had to quell the terror. It had him and it would kill him. There was nothing he could...

He drew both revolvers, jammed their muzzles into the creature's sides, and squeezed the triggers. The dual report was a muffled mess and he cried out when the claws already dug into his shoulders clenched and sank deeper into his flesh.

It dropped, lifeless, on top of him. A rush of air escaped the toothy mouth inches from his face. The reek of the rotting flesh caught between its sharp teeth made the Bounty Hunter gag. He rolled the creature off him and stood. Backing away, he combed a trembling hand through his sweaty hair. His eyes darted in their sockets.

What was this place? What the hell was that thing he just killed? Were there more of them?

And, if he didn't know any better, he'd think the creature was a dinosaur. Couldn't be though, right? Maybe the thing was just a big lizard of some sort. Trapped under the mountains, maybe it grew that way because of all the strange plants around.

So many maybes.

The Bounty Hunter loathed maybes.

He picked his hat up, snugged it onto his head and hunkered down beside the dead lizard creature to grab his rifle, which was lodged between him and the lizard and useless at the time. Before standing, he noted the single long talon on each foot of the creature. If either of those had got him, he would be dead now.

Luck.

He wasn't much to rely on luck, but knew it happened sometimes. He also knew when not to push it.

The Bounty Hunter stood, tipped his hat at the dead lizard creature, and set out to hunt down Scar and Bobby.

17

The heat of the place was worse than he'd ever experienced. So humid, at times, he could barely breathe. Worse than the tropics, as he moved deeper and deeper into the world under the mountains.

Although there were plenty of strange and frightening noises, he had yet to see another big lizard like what attacked him back by the stream. Eventually, though, he noticed a low, but steady hissing sound. Like a tea kettle before it screams.

Time passed and drenched in sweat, he decided to rest a bit before trying to track Scar. He didn't want to go back to the clearing and the stream, but he felt he might have missed some key tracks. Maybe they didn't take the easiest route out of the swamp and forged on through the muck.

Didn't make a lick of sense to the Bounty Hunter. Still, it wasn't like he had enough time to look anyway. From when he climbed into this strange world and being attacked by the big lizard creature, it felt like a mere blink.

One thing he wished he brought was his waterskin. Even if empty, the stream where the raccoon drank from looked clear enough. Pure spring water was his guess and right now it would be Heaven.

The Bounty Hunter was contemplating doubling back for water when the ground under him trembled. He wiped sweat from his forehead and snugged the hat on. He glanced around but didn't see anything more than trees and all that damn green.

The ground trembled again. This time, a bit stronger.

Again, the tremble. Again. Until the ground shook so much it was difficult to stand.

Something was approaching.

Something massive.

He spotted a tree with a large, dark trunk and slid behind it just as the monster broke through the trees in front of him. A few of the trees slammed to the ground mere feet from him to the right. Deep chuffing noises swelled in the humid air. A low growl rumbled.

The Bounty Hunter didn't move. He clutched the rifle against his chest and focused on breathing.

Not too loud. Easy now. Easy, or it'll hear you. If it hears you—

The ground quaked as the monster drew closer. The Bounty Hunter leaned against the tree, trying to keep his balance when a huge claw-like foot came down only a couple of feet away. Weeds and dirt spilled out from between thick talons. The tree he leaned against shook. The deep chuffing and growling went on for a good while and it took all the Bounty Hunter had not to run...or move for that matter.

Shiver after shiver passed through the Bounty Hunter. Fear. Something so foreign to him he wasn't quite sure what it was at first. Not the fear of getting shot or encountering a grizzly bear. No. This was a different kind of fear.

Dread...

The talons of the scaly foot wriggled for a second or two, then lifted out of sight.

It came down again a good twenty feet away, followed by the other clawed foot. Eventually, the quaking faded to nothing.

The Bounty Hunter blew out a sharp breath and collapsed to his knees in a thorny bramble. He didn't care. The thorns were small. The relief, however, was huge. The monster hadn't found him. Not in a long time had he felt like his six-year-old self, scared of the deeper shadows of his room late at night.

Eventually, he yanked himself out of the thorns and staggered to the giant claw print in the dirt. A print longer than he was tall and twice as wide. The monster had torn a ragged swath through the forest. Somewhere close, a bird, or God knew what else, chirped. He blinked at all the damage surrounding him and wondered what the hell could be so massive to create such destruction?

He didn't want to think on it too much, shook it off, and went about tracking down Scar and Bobby. The quicker he could lead them out of this strange world and kill them, the better. He'd strap them to their horses and collect the bounty. Everything would be peaches then. Maybe he'd be able to take a bit of time to go see his daughter, Ana.

Reality sunk in, however, as he moved away from the destruction and abruptly into the tall grass field. He stopped and backed out of the grass. It was so thick and tall anything could be hiding in there.

He was about to turn and go the other way when—

"Bobby? Ya there?"

The Bounty Hunter froze. He squinted at the tall grass.

"Shit," Scar said.

He wasn't far away, by the sound. Maybe fifteen or twenty feet straight ahead. The Bounty Hunter took a couple more paces backward and pointed the rifle at the grass in front of him. A bead of sweat trickled down the small of his back. The air was like trying to breathe through a wet cloth sack.

"Shh."

The Bounty Hunter's eyes widened, and he spun around just in time to catch a fist to his jaw. He dropped to a knee. A grunt escaped him and before he could stand again, another fist crashed into his nose. A crunch bashed through his head and he fell hard on his ass. Hot tears consumed his vision. Pain blasted through his head.

And yet, through it all, a quiet voice said, "That's for killin' m'brother, Wayne."

The Bounty Hunter barely had time to register this through the pounding agony in his face and head before another voice spoke up.

"Bashterd ish, mine…"

The Bounty Hunter managed to clear tears away enough to gape at the other Ramsy brother. Not Scar, but the one that should have been dead. He must have gone through the opening to this lost world before the other two. That's why the Bounty Hunter didn't see him before.

It wasn't Scar who was the leader of the gang, but…

The other Ramsy brother hunkered down in front of the Bounty Hunter. Most of the man's face was covered with blood-stained cloth wrappings.

"Thought ya killed me?"

The Bounty Hunter's hands stole to his nose and face. The pain tried to invade his mind and lose focus. Something he couldn't afford right now. So…he squeezed his nose and glared at the other Ramsy brother. The one held together with bloodstained cloths.

"Bullet pashed through m'shin'n' my nosh."

It took the Bounty Hunter, in his pain, to decipher what the man said: "Bullet passed through my chin and my nose."

Something like that, maybe?

He couldn't be sure, though went with it anyway.

"Nothin' worksh like b'fore but ya gonna feel worsh now."

The Bounty Hunter gaped at the other brother through his tears. His mind reeled. No one had ever gotten the drop on him like this before.

The Ramsy brother with the bloody rags holding his face together unsheathed a hunting knife and pressed the sharp side of the blade against the Bounty Hunter's cheek.

"Not yet, Johnny," Scar said and came huffing and puffing to hunker down beside his brother. "We gotta get outta this place first. Feel like I'm bein' hunted."

Johnny's cold green eyes squinted at the Bounty Hunter. "Take hish gunsh."

Scar leaned forward—

The ground trembled.

Scar froze, eyes wide. He glanced at Johnny.

"It'sh nothin'," Johnny said through the rags holding his face together. "Take them gunsh."

Scar frowned and leaned in to unbuckle the Bounty Hunter's belt.

Another tremble from the ground stopped him. Then another. And another. Each tremble growing stronger and more intense than the last.

Terror coiled around the Bounty Hunter like an icy serpent.

The monster. It was coming back. If they didn't hide, it might see them and...

Thud.

The trembles turned to quakes so strong both Ramsy brothers struggled to stand.

Bobby took hold of Scar's arm. "We need to leave. Now."

Scar shot Johnny a look and Johnny shook his head and pointed at the Bounty Hunter. "We let'im live he'll be comin' after ush."

"We don't leave now," Scar said, "whatever's comin' will eat us."

Johnny pointed the hunting knife at the Bounty Hunter. "We'll meetsh again."

All three scampered off into the forest, leaving the Bounty Hunter alone. He sagged away from the tree they had him pinned against, face in shards of agony. He rolled away as best he could, tore some of the tall grass out and buried himself under it.

Then…he waited for the monster lizard to sweep him up in its massive jaws and chomp him to bloody bits.

The quaking stopped. The same deep chuffing as before sounded. A low, grumbling growl…

The Bounty Hunter, despite his pain, lay as still as possible.

Heavy sniffing not far above him sent chills under his skin like thousands of tiny black spiders. Even so, he somehow found the strength not to get up and run. The strength to remain still. Either that, or he didn't have much strength at all. Not enough to move, let alone fight whatever creature wanted to eat him.

The pain leaked into weariness, however, and the Bounty Hunter's head rested in the dirt. He tried to force his eyes to stay open but…

18

Kisses.

Kisses on his right cheek.

Kisses from a long-lost lover. From…

Something cold pecked at his cheek. Something with a painful nip like an angry chickadee.

The Bounty Hunter woke and found himself covered in small, gray lizards. All about the size of a dove. Unlike actual lizards, though, these stood upright on two legs like the one that attacked him by the stream. The one pecking at his cheek, or rather, biting at it, hissed. The Bounty Hunter, heart racing, burst out of the tall grass on top of him and kicked away all the little creatures. He had to peel the one still nipping at his cheek off his shoulder. It writhed and squealed in his hand. Its slender neck snapped its narrow, bird-like head at him like a striking snake.

He never saw anything like it and threw it as far away from him as possible.

Its mates hopped and chirped around him like hungry chickens. He kicked them away again.

Scavengers, he thought. *Like coyotes or goddamn buzzards*.

They thought he was dead and would peck away at him before larger scavengers ambled along.

His skin lumped up like gooseflesh at the thought of larger scavengers.

Eventually, possibly after realizing their meal was far too alive to eat, the small creatures scattered into the deeper brush. The Bounty Hunter wheezed through his broken nose. One touch confirmed it too. Yep, broken. It was a good inch to the right from where it should have been.

He sat down, back against the nearest tree, placed his hands on either side of the canted nose, and wrenched it hard to the left. A loud crunch filled his skull. Agony surged through him so much so he bounced the back of his head off the tree a few times. An agony which lasted longer than before. Pain, it seemed, lingered the older he got.

The Bounty Hunter closed his eyes and let the pain ebb. If he tried to stand now, he would most likely lose balance and collapse to the ground. Images of Ana smiling shuffled through his mind. Of Michael's perplexed expression before the Bounty Hunter left him with Coy. Of his smiles before Coy. His thoughts, shuffling like playing cards through his mind. Ana. Michael. Over and over until...

He opened his eyes and, at first, his vision was nothing but a thick blur. Like trying to see through the muddy waters of the Maquoketa River back home.

When it cleared, he used the tree for balance and stood. It took a moment for everything to stop tilting and once it did, he staggered to a familiar claw print dug into the ground. Many, actually. Trees were toppled and uprooted. All the destruction, it reminded him of the tornado that tore through the nearest town and cut an ugly swath through his family's corn fields and ripped the cow barn into ragged pieces strewn in every direction.

A singular source of destruction.

That's what stomped through the forest. Something, mayhap, as big as a damn tornado and just as deadly. If not deadlier.

How something could grow to be so big, the Bounty Hunter didn't know.

A high-pitched sound came from his nose with every breath, which told him it wasn't set quite right. The pain was a dull roar, but at least manageable. He found his hat in one of the monster's tracks and snugged it on.

A quick glance around proved nothing. He needed water. That was the main thing. The Ramsy brothers could wait.

The Bounty Hunter, wheezing through a ruined nose, made his way deeper into the forest.

***

No water.

Every direction he tried, there wasn't a creek or pond.

No spring.

Nothing but walls of green surrounding him. Walls which seemed to inch closer and closer. Dense canopies loomed, able to snuff him out in an instant. Walls ready to crush and suffocate. Ready to silence him forever.

So, lost in this mindset, he didn't notice the rumbling of the ground under his boots, nor the occasional groans. He didn't notice cracking and snapping sounds.

He didn't notice anything until a loud crackling explosion threw him out of his thoughts.

And not a moment too soon.

The Bounty Hunter glanced over his shoulder in time to see something green and rather large blundering its way toward him. A hulking, brute of a beast. He dashed to the left, behind a thick tree and gaped while not one but two of the beasts rumbled by. The one closest groaned. A deep bass which shook the Bounty Hunter from the inside out. They looked so familiar too. Large heads with what appeared to be dark, curved beaks for mouths and three horns. Two long ones sprouted from its forehead, or thereabout, and another protruding from just behind the beak-like mouth. Something in the paper, perhaps.

A dinosaur...

They thundered through without incident. The earth shook, though not quite as bad as with the other creature.

And no matter how fast his heart beat he gathered a sense of calm from these creatures. A sense of peace. He leaned against the rough bark of the tree and watched them pass.

Dinosaurs. A word he had tried so hard to avoid since entering this lost world. A word always tugging at the fringes of his mind. Although the slim discovery of dinosaur fossils was still under scrutiny, there was no other explanation for what he had seen the moment he set foot here. But, if dinosaurs were all dead, how come they were still alive here under the mountains? Didn't make any sense. Was it possible the giant lizards were trapped down here for all those years?

It was almost too fantastical to believe.

And yet…

The giant lizards with horns lumbered away and the forest of green swallowed them up. In no time, even the rumbling stopped.

The Bounty Hunter blew out a long breath too heavy to be a sigh and decided to follow the two creatures. They should eventually lead him to water.

So, keeping to the thicker edges of their path, he followed.

He just hoped there would be water soon.

Before he got a chance to follow too far, though, something burst through the dense foliage and sprinted up the path toward the larger dinosaurs. It moved so fast the Bounty Hunter hardly got a good look at it. Moved faster than a cougar. He slowed and lifted his rifle a bit, though not attempting to shoot the creature.

Another slipped out of the brush on the other side of the path, nearly right beside the Bounty Hunter. It didn't even appear to notice him and hurried to catch up with its mate.

This time he got a better look and froze. His blood chilled and a shiver scuttled through him. It was the same kind of lizard creature as the one he had shot by the stream not long after setting foot in this lost world.

And still, another shot out of the bushes in front of him and raced up the path.

In the distance, a deep cry echoed.

Wolves, he thought. *They act like a pack of wolves.*

Only three so far, but yes, they were hunting their prey. How they intended to bring down suck large prey, though, was beyond the Bount —

At least six more shot out the bushes and ran up the path, leaving the Bounty Hunter gaping.

He stopped, rifle lowered, unable to move or think. All six at once. Six and all it would take was one to notice him and he'd be dead. Just—

It rammed into him with so much force he was driven to the ground. All air whooshed out of him and in a blink it was on top. Sharp pain lanced through his shoulders and he realized the creature had its talons dug into his shoulders. The Bounty Hunter cried out, kicking at the creature pinning him down. He brought the rifle up just in time for the large lizard's mouth to snap down on it, saving his face from being chomped off. Its curved, sharp teeth cut grooves through the metal and dug into the wood.

With a roar, he kicked the creature off him, aimed the rifle and fired.

The dinosaur was quick, though, and moved a hair before the Bounty Hunter squeezed the trigger. The shot went wild and the creature began to circle him like a hungry wolf. It hunched over, front claws splayed. A thin growl escaped from between its teeth. Its gray scaly skin folded some as the rear legs bent like tightly coiled springs.

Getting ready to pounce, the Bounty Hunter thought and cocked the rifle.

Ignoring the pain throughout his face and shoulders, the Bounty Hunter aimed the rifle. The dinosaur's crouch deepened.

"Don't do it, ya ugly bastard."

Its legs bent fully. Same as any animal about to pounce. Especially wolves and cougars. Or even eagles…

The Bounty Hunter fired and a smoldering hole no larger than a dime appeared between the large lizard's amber eyes. Eyes which rolled up to reveal only the whites before the creature collapsed.

A sigh flowed out of the Bounty Hunter. He lowered the rifle and staggered away. With the dinosaur dead all the pain came rushing back in again. Well, at least he thought it was a dinosaur. Nothing like he'd ever read about, unlike the ones with the three horns. What were they called again? Tri…something. He couldn't rightly remember.

The wounds in his shoulders weren't as deep as he thought they were. He had worse gouges from a black bear attack years ago. Hurt like hell, though. The creature must not have gotten a good hold on him. If it had…if those talons sunk deep into the muscle and bone…

He'd be dead.

Making sure to replace the bullet he spent on the dinosaur, the Bounty Hunter cocked the rifle and continued up the broken path.

19

Staggering, unable to keep himself standing any longer, the three horned dinosaurs finally stopped at what appeared to be a lake for a drink.

The Bounty Hunter found a space under a thick bush and nearly collapsed. Everything hurt. The thick, humid air made it so hard to breathe all he could do was lie there in the scant weeds under the bush and shiver. He needed water. He needed time to rest both his mind and body. Just a smidge of time.

A roar exploded through the damp air and he scrambled farther under the bush. The ground quaked. Something shrieked. The Bounty Hunter, heart trip-hammering, rolled as deep as he could under the bush until everything but a narrow view to the beach of the lake was visible.

Boom.

Boom.

The quaking of something enormous mingled with the wary thuds of the three horned dinosaurs. Round feet like that of an elephant struck the ground as they turned to look for whatever was approaching.

They splashed into the lake, leapt out and paced the beach.

Why aren't they running? The Bounty Hunter shifted a bit so he could see better and all the blood in him froze.

Smaller dinosaurs were closing in from the left while the same amount moved in from the right. The same ones he saw sprint up the path not long ago, no doubt. The very same kind he killed two of so far. As tall as two turkeys stacked on top of each other. Sharp, curved teeth and long, hook-like claws. The much larger, three horned dinosaurs only had two options. Run into the lake and quite possibly drown, or back into the forest where something big approached.

The smaller dinosaurs were like a pack of wolves the way they moved. Almost like they wanted their prey scared before attacking. Packs all worked differently, he knew. Some tended to play with their food first while others went for the kill right away. The smaller dinosaurs appeared to be the former.

Ground shaking under him, the Bounty Hunter took aim with his rifle at one of the smaller creatures. He would need to be quick after the first shot. As soon as they knew where he was, they'd all pounce on him at once. He'd be dead before he had time to gasp.

On his stomach, he set his sights on the nearest meat eater. He blew out a slow breath, right index finger slowly squeezing the trigger. He couldn't rush it. If he did—

Massive jaws swung down and snatched one of the small meateater's up. Blood burst in all directions, then the monster lifted the smaller dinosaur out of view. The others squeaked and scattered. One leaped right over the Bounty Hunter and scurried into the dense brush.

Heart bashing against his ribs, the Bounty Hunter gained a knee and peered out of the heavy foliage. The two three-horned dinosaurs bumped into each other, brayed and hissed. Both of them looked up at something the Bounty Hunter still couldn't see because of the thick canopy. Bloody bits and pieces of the smaller dinosaur rained down and thumped onto the yellow sand of the beach.

The Bounty Hunter, every sinew screaming for him to run, raised the rifle toward the canopy.

Silence spread throughout the forest, even the two three-horned dinosaurs fell quiet. Their frantic bumping, thrashing, and bellowing stopped. They looked around, large nostrils near their beaks expanding as they sniffed the air.

The Bounty Hunter released a pent-up breath he didn't know he'd been holding. Maybe the giant creature left? He didn't feel it go, but that didn't mean anything. He was so amped up he—

A large claw-foot crashed down mere feet away from him. Sand burst into the air. He turned away, coughing. The grit in his mouth and face was enough to drive him to stab an innocent lamb. He spat and sputtered, trying to get the sand out of his mouth. He wiped at his eyes to try and clear them. A deafening roar quaked the very air around him. One of the three-horned dinosaurs shrieked.

The Bounty Hunter, clearing the last of what he could from his eyes, spun around, lifted the rifle and—

Froze.

A huge, long snouted lizard face glared at him from no more than three feet away. So large, it reminded him of the dragons in fairy tale paintings. Its scaly nostrils flared. Hot, foul air blew into him as the creature took in his scent. Deep clicks sounded from either its mouth or throat. Long, pointy teeth curved slightly out from under its top jaw and lay starkly exposed on its lower jaw. The very sight drove spears of icy terror into the Bounty Hunter's gut and chest. Those foot-long teeth. The way it appeared to study him. And what was he to think but death? Surely, it was his time.

Still, terror gripped him in cold claws and refused to release him. They wanted him to bear witness, those proverbial claws. They wanted him to fully realize he wasn't above. No. He was below, stuck below the mountains with ravenous dinosaurs.

Whether he liked it or not, this was the reality he found himself in.

A massive foul breath blew from those scaly nostrils, knocking the hat off the Bounty Hunter's head. A deep growl shook the air, sending his heart into a flurry of beats. His stomach churned at the stench radiating from the creature. Rotting meat was the only thing his terrified mind could latch onto. There were other sickening scents laced through it, but he didn't care to identify them. What mattered was the monstrosity before him. A creature out of time. Not one of the small guys, but the reason why so many youngsters were enthralled by dinosaurs.

This was one of the big guys, though he wasn't so sure if it was like the one he heard of being dug up in Montana. Paper claimed it was a big son of a bitch too, though excavation could take a couple of years those scientists folk claimed, he reckoned they might never know what it was hiding in all that rock and dirt.

A bead of sweat trickled down the side of his face and for a second or two, an unsettling calm swept over everything. Him. The massive dinosaur. All green surrounding them.

The Bounty Hunter steeled himself, leapt to the right, pointed the rifle at the monster's dark, green eye, and pulled the trigger. It reared, a howl like no other exploded from its mouth. He landed hard on his side, stood and looked up.

The giant dinosaur staggered, clawing at its injured eye. Blood poured down the side of its green, scaly head. Its claw-like feet stamped the beach, creating a flurry of sand.

The Bounty Hunter cocked the rifle. He had about thirteen bullets left in the weapon. All of them he planned on using to take down the creature.

The eyes, he thought. *Keep shooting its eyes*.

He aimed but the monster shifted away, stomping its feet and roaring. Sand rushed over the Bounty Hunter in a yellow wave. He spun away, though the sheer force of it shoved him to his knees. The ground quaked enough to toss him onto his stomach. Sputtering, he struggled to gain his feet, but failed and fell. He just couldn't find the strength. Flashes of his Ana stuttered before his mind's eye. The tears on her face when he left her for the West years ago. Then but a young girl. Her hands reaching out for him as the midwife and caretaker held her back.

As he set out to make a better life for them both.

How many years had it been?

Far too long…

He saw Michael. His face void of emotion at first before turning up into a smile. Then, much like Ana, confused and teary when he needed to leave. Coy…the kind, old, Comanche, steering the boy away and into the cave…

The Bounty Hunter burst out of the sand in a coughing fit. He rolled onto his side and spat sand. He whooped in a breath, coughed some more and collapsed onto his back. Above, the canopy was dark green. No sun in the sky and yet it was clear as day out.

It took a few tries, but the Bounty Hunter managed to sit up.

The three-horned dinosaurs were gone and, from what he could tell, so was the monstrous one. He sat, gathering his thoughts while the world around him lightly rumbled.

Rumbled…

He frowned. He hadn't noticed any rumbling before. Unless it was so minor, and with everything else going on, his senses just didn't pick up on it. Nothing threatening. Just a minor, constant rumble. A mellow background noise, really. Something noticed, though easily ignored.

The Bounty Hunter grabbed his hat and stood. His legs trembled a bit, but held, thank God. Rifle in hand, he made his way onto the beach. Avoiding all the deep tracks pounded into the sand, he walked to the lake, dropped to his knees and cupped his hands under the water.

He might get sick, but he didn't care. He needed water. Needed it more so than anything right now. If he wanted to live, it was either drink the lake water or die slowly.

So, the Bounty Hunter brought his cupped hands full of lake water up and slurped down a mouthful. He lowered his hands and waited. Nothing about the taste was off. Nothing foul or too minerally. Clean was the word which first sprang into his mind. Though he had drunk from what he thought was a clean well before and lay sick for weeks after. Without taking time to boil, he took his chances.

The water wouldn't make him sick immediately, so he strolled the beach and waited. The toes of his boots kicked up strange shells. Each one more colorful and oddly shaped than the last. More than a few were round with squiggly appendages like thin tentacles, though everything was solid. Some were gnarled masses of purple and yellow. Whatever lived in such shells defied his imagination.

Gradually, the forest around him came back to life. First with a squeak—something deep in the fauna to his left—then hoots and squawks. Before long, the dim rumbling he heard before was drowned out.

He followed the three-horned dinosaurs' tracks for a time down the beach before they cut back into the forest where they could hide better. The Bounty Hunter smiled and knelt at the shoreline. He scooped up some more lake water and drank. So far, illness hadn't found him yet. Maybe a slight quiver in his guts, but that was to be expected after not having water for so long. Still, he waited. He strode the beach. Back and forth. His thoughts wandered from Ana to Michael, to Coy and where the Ramsy brothers could be hiding.

What if they decided to leave me to the dinosaurs? The Bounty Hunter frowned out over the lake, which was quite vast, he noted. *What if they're already on their way to Montana or gone south?*

He could double back. Hell, he could leave this place and not bat an eye. The only snag was the possibility of the Ramsy brothers. If one escaped, he might be okay. But both? No. He needed the payment. He needed to ensure Ana would be in good care until he returned. There was no questioning it.

His gaze fixed on a large, white cloud which stretched the entire length of the lake and then some. He reckoned it had to be miles long for it disappeared into the glowing horizon.

The Bounty Hunter drank some more from the lake and went looking for the Ramsy brothers.

20

He followed the tawny beach, sparing time to drink more lake water, then set out into the forest again.

He—

Something dark crashed into him, though not hard enough to knock him over. He spun and—

Bobby, tiny scratches all over his face, eyes wide and wild, drew a knife and lunged.

The Bounty Hunter sidestepped, though not quick enough and Bobby's blade sliced a gash into the Bounty Hunter's left forearm. He deflected another attack with his rifle and punched Bobby square in the face with enough force to send the younger man flailing.

"Stop," the Bounty Hunter said. "My bounty is not for you."

Bobby, however, didn't appear to hear or refused to care. Either or, he lunged again with the knife. And again. The Bounty Hunter smacked each advance away with his rifle. The boy was mad. Lost his mind in a lost world. Those wild eyes. Always shifting and never remaining on the Bounty Hunter for long. Didn't take away from the attacks and lunges, though.

"Bobby," the Bounty Hunter said. "Stop! Now! I am not after you!"

Still, Bobby struck out with that dagger of his. Yes. A dagger. Not a hunting or skinning knife. The blade was designed to kill people, not skin animals. Made to stab into the neck, stomach, sides or chest. Quick, but deadly stabs to a person.

The Bounty Hunter smacked Bobby's dagger away with the barrel of his rifle once more.

There was no sanity in the younger man's eyes.

Bobby lunged again and the Bounty Hunter spun, whacked the knife out of the assassin's hand and swung around, cracking the back of Bobby's head with the butt of the rifle. The boy dropped like a sack of potatoes.

The Bounty Hunter kneeled, and rolled Bobby over. The kid was still breathing. Good. There was no money on Bobby, and, despite the boy's choices, the Bounty Hunter would not claim him. Well, unless he was forced to. Then so be it.

Bobby, however, was out cold.

One of the small, gray dinosaurs which tried to eat him in what felt like a decade ago, leaped out of a patch of tall grass.

The Bounty Hunter glanced from it to all the scratches on Bobby's haggard face and back again.

"So, you're the bastards that drove him mad."

The small dinosaur, lizard, whatever, chittered at the Bounty Hunter. It was cute, in its own, weird way. Almost warranted a petting like a cat or dog. He went to do just that when the small dinosaur pounced and latched itself onto his face and knocked his hat off. Tiny talons dug into his scalp. Its teeth snipped at his eyes. Yes, the Bounty Hunter could see why Bobby went mad. He imagined one after another latching onto the man. Dozens. All of them clawing and biting and growling their tiny growls over and over in his ears...

The Bounty Hunter yanked the critter off his face, threw it to the ground and stomped on its bird-like head until it stopped moving.

He waited, but there were no more little gray scavengers. He tossed the carcass of the one he killed into the weeds and went about setting up a small camp. He could use a bit of a rest to collect his thoughts. No fire, though. Nothing to attract either the Ramsy brothers or larger dinosaurs. The Bounty Hunter propped Bobby up against a tree and took the waterskin tied to his belt. He filled the skin up at the lake and when he returned, Bobby was making thick groaning sounds.

The Bounty Hunter hunkered down in front of the younger man and uncorked the water skin. "I have some water. Drink." He nudged the brim of the waterskin on Bobby's chapped bottom lip.

The man sucked in a sharp breath. His eyes opened, closed, opened and he surged forward.

The Bounty Hunter slammed Bobby back against the tree, angry now. He got within inches of the man's greasy face.

"Listen, ya little bastard. I'm not gonna kill'ya. If I wanted to, I'd have done it when you were out. You're not my bounty." He shoved the waterskin at Bobby. Water splashed out onto the younger man's chest. "Now drink."

Bobby, chest heaving with every breath, eyes still a bit wild, glanced from the Bounty Hunter to the water held to his chest. His cracked lips quivered, though no words came out. He upended the waterskin, sucking down gulp after gulp. Water trickled down his whiskered chin and dripped to the ground.

The Bounty Hunter took the waterskin from Bobby. "That's enough for now. Don't want ya gettin' sick."

Bobby glowered at the Bounty Hunter. "What do y'want? Ya killed my brother, Wayne."

"Well, now," the Bounty Hunter said, "I am sorry about that. I was hired to gather the Ramsy brothers, not kill anyone, but, as ya know…some killin' happens."

Bobby's green eyes narrow. "So, you're really a bounty hunter." Not really a question.

"Yup. The Ramsy brothers are going to keep my daughter warm and fed."

For the first time, Bobby revealed real emotion. His scowl switched to a frown.

"Ya got a daughter?"

"Yup."

Bobby leaned forward and took the waterskin from the Bounty Hunter's hand and knocked back a swig. He leaned back against the tree and tentatively touched one of the deeper gashes on his face. A four-inch cut running from the bottom lobe of his ear to about the corner of his mouth. He sucked in a sharp breath through his teeth and shivered.

"They got me pretty bad, I guess."

"Yup."

The Bounty Hunter relaxed some. Maybe Bobby wasn't as insane as he appeared at first go. Initially, perhaps, but not so much now. Being attacked and stalked by small, meat eating dinosaurs would drive anyone mad, the Bounty Hunter reckoned.

He let Bobby take a few more pulls on the waterskin and placed his hat on his head. "Where are they?"

Bobby snorted. "Ya really think I'm gonna tell ya that?"

The Bounty Hunter smiled, shot forward, knocked the waterskin out of Bobby's hands and jammed the muzzle of his rifle under Bobby's scruffy chin. "I reckon I do. You're gonna tell me where they're holed up or I'll put a hole in your goddamn head."

But Bobby only laughed. His bloodshot eyes fixed on the Bounty Hunter. Wide and wild again.

"I ain't your bounty. Said so yerself. Ya won't kill me."

The Bounty Hunter's jaw clenched. A sigh wheezed through his broken nose. "Last chance." He cocked the rifle.

Still, Bobby chuckled. His wide, bloodshot eyes darted. "Ya won't make it outta here alive, Bounty Hunter. Either the brothers will get ya or—"

A claw, about as long as the Bounty Hunter was tall, smacked into the tree a few inches above Bobby's head. Slivers and chunks of bark fell into the young man's mop of black hair. His wide eyes, now even wider, snapped to look at the Bounty Hunter. Dark talons dug deep grooves into the side of the tree as the claw pulled away. Three gashes in all.

The Bounty Hunter rolled away, stood and pointed the rifle upward. A long jawed, toothy grin greeted him. The massive dinosaur which seemed to be stalking him the entire time. Its green eye narrowed on him. The other was a bloody ruin where he'd shot it.

It's toying with us, he thought. *Like a fat cat with a mouse.*

Then Bobby screamed and the creature's attention shifted away from the Bounty Hunter.

Run. Run and hide while it's distracted.

But the Bounty Hunter did not move. Instead, he moved around until the perfect shot came around. Right at the creature's remaining good eye.

A growl shook the air and before the Bounty Hunter could shoot, the giant dinosaur dipped down and snapped Bobby between its jaws. Only his top half, though. His legs kicked while the creature stepped back and shook its head vigorously. The lower half of Bobby was torn from his body and went flying, legs still kicking.

How did the giant lizard creature sneak up on them without shaking the ground like before?

Or had it been in the same area the entire time? Maybe it was waiting for the perfect time to seek vengeance on the Bounty Hunter. Were dinosaurs capable of revenge? He wasn't so sure...

The color of the creature was covered in shades of grays and greens.

The worst part was listening to Bobby scream. The man was still alive. Probably punching the inside of the dinosaur's mouth while it reared and swallowed him. It was in that space of silence when the Bounty Hunter stepped around the tree the giant creature cut grooves into, aimed, and fired his rifle.

The bullet hit its target dead-on. The creature's remaining eye burst and burped blood and whitish goo from the eye socket. Its claws slapped the side of its head like it was trying to swat away a pesky insect. Its elongated mouth, which reminded the Bounty Hunter of those things called alligators from the swampy south of America, opened wide without a sound. It staggered to the right, toward the lake, stopped and staggered left. Its massive jaws snapped shut with a loud, hollow *thock*.

Something like a whine drifted from the monster while it staggered back and forth. While it toppled trees and bashed the sandy dirt into oblivion with its huge, claw-like feet. Things that looked like something crossed between a turkey and a Gila monster. Shaped like a turkey foot but scaly like a lizard. The Bounty Hunter backed away as the monstrous thing swayed and snapped its huge jaws. Its claws dug at its bloody eye sockets, slashing scales and skin to ribbons until, finally, it let loose a roar so loud it deafened the Bounty Hunter.

Gobbets of blood-soaked flesh rained down. The Bounty Hunter kept moving backward, distancing himself from the monster and still got pummeled with ragged bits of flesh. It stank, those bits and pieces. Not of rotting meat, but something dank. Like a moldy bundle of cloth forgotten under a sink.

The heel of his right boot caught a raised tree root and he fell hard on his butt. A spike of pain stabbed up his back, but he'd worry about that later. He needed to get away. He needed to run. Because, if that big bastard fell on him it'd be the end of everything. Squished, like a bug.

But the dinosaur didn't fall. Instead, it staggered and stomped, toppling trees and kicking up clouds of sandy earth.

The Bounty Hunter was so focused on the monster, he didn't feel the cold steel of a gun barrel pressed against his cheek until it gave a firm nudge.

He froze. His heart stuttered. Of all the things…

"Don't move." The voice was mushy. Had to be Johnny. "Or I'll blow your gsh'damn head cleansh off."

The giant dinosaur roared and staggered closer. Trees snapped and pummeled to the ground a few yards from the Bounty Hunter. The ground shook so much it took extra effort for him to remain standing.

"Thish way," Johnny said and pulled on the Bounty Hunter's arm.

The Bounty Hunter dropped; Johnny fired. The sound was just as deafening as the monster dinosaur's roar. There wasn't time to think.

He dropped to his knees, shoved the muzzle of his rifle at Johnny's right knee, and pulled the trigger.

Blood misted the air and the Ramsy brother dropped, clutching his injured knee. He screamed. The strips of skin keeping his face together ripped.

They were worth more alive…

The Bounty Hunter glanced from the dinosaur to Johnny Ramsy. Where was Scar?

No time to worry about it now, the dinosaur was getting too close. In a couple more staggers it'd be on top of them and more than likely crush them both.

"Shit," the Bounty Hunter said, grabbed the collar of Johnny's vest and dragged the man through the dense forest.

Johnny never stopped screaming.

21

The monstrosity stumbled toward the lake, but the Bounty Hunter continued dragging Johnny deeper into the woods. He needed to find a place to hide the man until he rounded up Scar. The only issue was how to keep Johnny in one place long enough for all that.

The main thing right now, however, was getting as far away from the blind dinosaur as possible. If Johnny hadn't stopped him, he would have ended the creature's suffering. Well, at least tried.

The trees and all the green foliage thinned, and the Bounty Hunter found himself walking over small, dark brown rocks. Rocks that were nearly red. They crunched under his boots and the air stank of rotten eggs. Not only this, the air felt warmer. Not by a little, but a lot. The entire area, for as far as he could see beyond where he stood, glowed bright orange and red. Almost so bright he had to turn away.

He stopped dragging Johnny.

"Bashterd," Johnny shouted. "Shot me!"

The Bounty Hunter hunkered down in front of the man. "Still alive, ain't ya? Where's your brother?"

Johnny, face in a hue of orange, grinned. "Comin' for ya now." Johnny cackled laughter and the Bounty Hunter punched him hard enough to knock the guy out.

He leaned Johnny against a tree, its gray bark peeling. From just a few feet back into the forest the Bounty Hunter found a few thin vines he cut free and piled near the unconscious outlaw. Then he took a few minutes to survey his surroundings.

The area he stood in was hotter than the desert. In the horizon there appeared to be the source of the immense glow which radiated off the rocks and created a domelike curvature high in the sky. The light from the single source, it appeared, illuminated the rest of the badlands.

Such a strange place.

A place, he knew, should not exist.

The Bounty Hunter tied the vines around Johnny, holding him to the tree, and sat down on a log to think and rest his weary legs. More so to rest. His entire body ached. Bruises, cuts, scrapes. Broken nose. A battered body inching into its fortieth year. Not old. Not young. Somewhere in between.

All around him were sounds. Some he couldn't place; others reminded him of birds. But, as far as he could remember, he hadn't seen any birds here. At least, not yet. There was just too much happening to care. Now, though, he took a moment to listen. Even if he couldn't see them, they were there. Somewhere high up in all those tall, strange trees.

Johnny groaned, though didn't lift his mutilated head.

It still confused the Bounty Hunter how the man lived with an obliterated face.

His mother always told him evil found a way to survive, and, before long, the Bounty Hunter knew it to be true. Evil always found a way…

The Bounty Hunter stood. All he needed to do was roundup Scar. If he could bring both brothers in alive the pay would be more than his troubles. He hunkered down in front of Johnny. Only tatters of the cloth holding his face together remained. The man did not move. His narrow chest rose and fell with every breath. His eyes lolled behind closed eyelids.

No, he wouldn't leave Johnny tied up and alone. Not here. Not in a place where practically everything wanted to eat you.

You get paid even if he's dead, a small voice spoke up in the Bounty Hunter's head.

Yeah, but he would get more if they were both alive. Enough, perhaps, to set aside the bounty hunting and gunslinging. He was mulling this over when something crashed into him hard enough to knock the wind out of his lungs.

The Bounty Hunter rolled, gasping for air. Something screeched. The ground trembled. He managed to drag himself into a small thicket, still gasping, and turn enough to see what hit him. Another dinosaur. This one was larger than the first that attacked him, though way smaller than the gargantuan he shot the eyes out of. A beak, similar to an eagle, curved down the front of its mouth. The rest of its head was large and oval shaped. Small horns surrounded the crest. It snorted and stomped the ground, kicking up dirt and the red rocks. But it wasn't looking at the Bounty Hunter, nor Johnny, who still slept.

No. It was spooked by something and glanced around frantically. It mewled and stomped.

A deep, rattling growl stopped the creature's frenzy. Indeed, it about stopped the Bounty Hunter's heart just as he was catching his breath. The dinosaur with the oval head and beak blinked upward at something the Bounty Hunter couldn't see.

Rifle in hand, he moved deeper into the thicket. Thorns snagged his shirt and cut his skin, but he didn't care. Something big was hunting the smaller dinosaur and it couldn't be the one without eyes. Or could it? Maybe he missed one of the eyes with a shot and the monster was hunting him now.

No. Both eyes were shot out, but—

Massive jaws snapped over the top half of the smaller dinosaur and lifted it into the air. The Bounty Hunter followed it upward and, through the brambles, gaped at another large dinosaur, though not quite as big as the one he shot the eyes out of. This one appeared to be mostly deadly jaws as it shook the smaller dinosaur back and forth until the lower half tore away. The big dinosaur reared and swallowed the upper half without pause. The small arms of the large creature lashed at the air with dual talons for claws. It stepped out of the forest to eat the rest of the smaller dinosaur.

Big back legs. Long tail. Tan colored skin. A few feathers adorned the very back of its head in a frilly spray of gray.

"Oh," Johnny said, staring up at the creature. "Oh, Hell."

The dinosaur, however, didn't pay the mangled man any mind. Rather, it feasted on the remains of the smaller creature. Which took as long as it did for the Bounty Hunter to aim his rifle at it. There was nowhere to go and if it saw him, he probably wouldn't live through it. Unlike the other monster, this one appeared to be faster and less hesitant to attack. Maybe its brain was smaller. Maybe different hunting styles. He didn't know. All he knew was to be ready.

Johnny kicked his legs, trying to thrash and escape the vines holding him to the tree. His eyes were wide and thin whines spewed from his ruined face, mingling with the hissing and low rumblings from the distance. Johnny's head whipped from side to side, unfurling most of the tattered cloth holding his face together. Scabs broke open and blood soaked the remaining cloth. What was under it all became a howling horror the Bounty Hunter could not look at without feeling sick. How the man was still alive was beyond him.

The big dinosaur with the big head and small arms pivoted and was about to move away when Johnny began to scream and broke through one of the vines holding him. A part of the vine whipped outward and smacked the creature's leg. It stopped in mid stride and stepped back around to the tree. It lowered its huge head and stared directly at Johnny.

Johnny shrieked and thrashed. He kicked his legs. A bit of his lower jaw waggled about as he whipped his head back and forth in the struggle.

The dinosaur drew in a breath and huffed it out through nostrils the size of the Bounty Hunter's fists, ruffling Johnny's sweaty, dark hair. The man tried to kick the creature, but it was no use. He couldn't quite get high enough with his boot. Then, all Johnny could do was scream. He gave up thrashing and—

Something smacked onto the Bounty Hunter's upper back, claws sinking in like fishhooks. A tiny growl trembled the air not far from his right ear. Then it sank its teeth into his shoulder. He gritted his teeth, trying to ignore the pain, and reached around to yank the creature off him when it snipped onto a finger.

"Bastard," he said and reached around with his other hand, this time lower.

He grabbed what felt like a tail and pulled until the small creature squealed. Instead of letting go, however, the little son of a bitch dug in more. The pain was getting almost unbearable. He tried several times to reach behind him and rip the thing off him when a gust of hot air blew the hat off his head.

The Bounty Hunter's heart stuttered. He stopped trying to pull the small creature off, no doubt one of the small dinosaurs that about drove Bobby mad, and turned to come face to toothy mouth with the big dinosaur. A deep growl emanated from it. The fist-sized nostrils widened, drawing in the Bounty Hunter's scent. He moved aside to avoid most of the exhale.

A mistake.

The monster's jaws opened wide and an explosive roar rocked him. He flailed backward, nearly forgetting the small creature on his back still chewing and clawing away. The big dinosaur lunged. Its eight-inch teeth snapped about two inches from his face.

The Bounty Hunter pointed the rifle at the open mouth and fired.

The creature whined, reared back. It shook its head and lunged at the Bounty Hunter again. He fired another shot, but those massive jaws snapped down on the barrel of his rifle before he could see if there was any damage. All it took was a hard yank and the monster had his rifle. It moved away enough to swallow it down whole like a blue herring.

"Sonofabitch," the Bounty Hunter said all in one word and drew his right revolver.

The thing still clawed and bit into his back. The pain was getting so bad tears threatened to blur his vision. He wiped them quickly and ran from the thicket into the forest. Johnny howled something at him, but the Bounty Hunter didn't stop. At the first tree, he swung around and slammed his back against it as hard as he could, crushing the little monster between him and the tree.

It gave a short yip, then the claws digging into the Bounty Hunter's back fell away. The creature dropped to the ground. Wincing with the pain in his back, the Bounty Hunter turned and glared at the thing while it twitched in the weeds. He brought his boot heel down on its head several times until he heard the crunch of its tiny skull.

But, in his desperation to be free of the small dinosaur digging into his back, he forgot—

It crashed through the trees, charging at him with its cavernous mouth wide open and roaring.

The Bounty Hunter fired a couple of bullets into that mouth and leapt aside. He fell hard on his shoulder, stood, and spun just as the dinosaur's jaws snapped around a tree next to him.

"Shit," he said and ran.

Behind him, the creature roared.

The Bounty Hunter didn't stop running. He couldn't stop. Johnny be damned.

22

The Bounty Hunter ran until he collapsed near a pile of boulders. There appeared to be a small opening, no wider than four feet, between two of the largest boulders.

Exhausted, body racked with pain, he dragged himself into the opening as far as he could. Somewhere in the distance, the dinosaur with the big head and little arms roared. But that was far away. His body simply couldn't move anymore. Too much. It was just too...

Darkness swept over him in a quiet wave and gently coaxed him into the sea of sleep.

***

In the depths of sleep, someone shouted a name over and over. The voice echoed through the dark waters where the Bounty Hunter rested. Over and over. The same name. Louder...louder.

The Bounty Hunter's eyes opened to slits as the dark depths of sleep receded.

"Johnny," a man shouted. "*Johnny!*"

The Bounty Hunter drew in a breath and coughed from inhaling dust. He rolled onto his side. Inside the opening between the boulders was too dark to see. He barely remembered dragging himself in here. Pain pulsed through his back and he dreaded what kind of damage the little bastard had done. He would need to find a doctor of some sort after all this. Some stitching was in order.

His grunts and breathing echoed throughout the small space while he shifted enough to see out the opening. Nothing but the green of the forest beyond. No more did he hear the roaring of the dinosaur with the big head and feathers. Only the man shouting over and over.

"Johnny!"

Scar, the Bounty Hunter thought and checked the cylinder of his revolver. Three bullets. Wincing with every move, he reloaded the gun and pointed it toward the opening. Scar sounded close. Right outside. All the man would have to do was kneel and he'd see the Bounty Hunter. With nowhere to go, the Bounty Hunter knew he'd be dead as soon as Scar began firing. Regardless, the Bounty Hunter's vision remained that of the forest.

"Johnny! Where the hell are ya?" Scar's voice cracked on the word hell.

If Johnny was still alive, it would be a miracle, especially how ravenous all the dinosaurs seemed to be.

"Johnny!"

Farther away now.

The Bounty Hunter sighed and crawled out from between the boulders. He gritted his teeth against the throbbing pain all over his back. His face and broken nose ached and all he wanted to do was find a bed and sleep for hours.

Still, he carried on, following the shouts like breadcrumbs.

Scar would need to be captured before going to check on Johnny (and get his hat back) so not to waste too much time. Whoops and tweets filled the forest and he still wasn't sure if they were birds or something else. Too high up. But if there were raccoons in this lost world, then surely there could be birds. Right?

"Johnny!"

Barely above the noises of the forest now.

The Bounty Hunter didn't holster his gun. Not with how unpredictable this world was. Anything could leap out at him at any time and he'd rather have his gun at the ready than scrambling to draw the damn thing. He quickened his step, knowing he needed to get to Scar before a dinosaur did. And with the man bellowing like that, no doubt something heard.

"Johnny! Where ya at, brother?"

Closer. The Bounty Hunter fell into a light jog.

Something rustled in the brush to his left, but he refused to stop running. Whatever it was, maybe it would lose interest, or just a spooked raccoon. Either or, he didn't stop. The forest swished by him while he dipped and dodged low hanging branches and smaller trees. Scar wasn't far. Just a few more—

The largest cat the Bounty Hunter had ever seen leapt out of the forest in front of him. It screamed like a cougar, only much deeper. Two of its front teeth protruded from its open mouth and curved down a foot past its white, furry chin.

The Bounty Hunter skidded to a stop and pointed his revolver at the beast. It was as large as a buffalo, though definitely a cat of some kind.

The beast scream-roared at him again, stubby ears back and flat against its head. It flashed all its teeth in a growl and shifted its stance. The big cat began moving to the right. Its green gaze never left the Bounty Hunter. A constant growl rumbled in its thick throat.

The Bounty Hunter's heart tumbled over itself while his mind tried to think of a plan. Something. Anything. How many shots would it take to kill the massive cat? Take out its eyes like the gigantic creature with the long mouth? The way the thing moved, though, he wasn't sure he could shoot out its eyes so easily. The way it moved was different. Very catlike rather than lizard-like. Or birdlike. Everything was refined and sleek. It moved like water. Each step was deliberate, furthering its agenda.

Its eyes narrowed.

A bead of sweat trickled down the side of the Bounty Hunter's face as the cat-beast circled. His heart gave a flurry of beats. The way it moved; the Bounty Hunter found it more difficult to take a shot. Because, what if he missed? Or what if he merely wounded it? A grizzly bear was more apt to tear you to ribbons if they were shallowly wounded. Like a bee sting, the Bounty Hunter assumed. A mild flesh wound would irritate and escalate rather than deter.

So...the Bounty Hunter waited for his shot.

A deep growl rumbled in its throat. It flashed its big teeth and circled, head lowered, green eyes motionless in their sockets. He kept his gaze fixed on it, ready for the slightest shift. Everything about it screamed speed. Like a mountain lion. Swift and purposeful unless it was merely trying to scare you off.

This beast, however, wanted its dinner. It was not trying to scare him away. Indeed, it chose him for the main course.

The Bounty Hunter kept the gun pointed at it while they did a clumsy dosey doe. He—

It pounced. This large beast of a cat.

The Bounty Hunter didn't have time to jump away and instead dropped to a knee and fired six quick shots into the beast-cat's exposed chest and face. He ducked, though not quite enough. The beast caught his upper body and shoved him along with it. The world became a topsy-turvy mess. Pain stabbed and smacked at him from every angle. When it all came to a rest, he found himself struggling for air.

With it on top of him, the Bounty Hunter was suffocating. He punched and kicked at it. He tried wriggling out from underneath, but the beast was too heavy.

This is it, he thought. *Can't breathe.*

He pushed at the thing with everything he had, but it would not budge.

This is it...

The Bounty Hunter let go his final breath.

I'm so sorry, Ana. I tried.

His mind grew fuzzy around the edges. Red pulsed behind his closed eyelids. There was no pain, just this sense of loss. Of being lulled into Death's bony arms. Knowledge of dying, though without any drama. Like a candle being snuffed out, the Bounty Hunter…

He sucked in a sharp breath of air and blinked at the red-tinged canopy.

Smacking sounds rolled into him one by one. Trying to breathe, he crawled away from the sound. It did not matter if he could breathe now. Whatever was munching on the giant cat, he imagined, held no qualms about slurping him up too. He found some dense brush and dragged himself into it. Now he just hoped the thing didn't see him…

The Bounty Hunter moved so he could see better and all the air he managed to take in leaked out of his lungs again.

The creature eating the giant cat was the massive dinosaur. The one with the elongated mouth and big teeth.

The one he shot both eyes out of.

Blood still leaked from the empty eye sockets.

The Bounty Hunter reloaded his revolver, snapped the cylinder in place and thumbed the hammer back.

"Johnny!"

The Bounty Hunter's heart skipped a beat. The monstrous dinosaur swallowed down the rest of the beast-cat and cocked its head.

"Johnny, that you? Heard shots!"

A deep rumbling growl emanated from the dinosaur.

"Brother! Say something!"

The massive dinosaur reared and turned in the direction of Scar's voice. Blood dripped from its lower jaw. Fur coated its exposed teeth.

"Johnny?"

The dinosaur backed into denser brush until only its muzzle and nostrils were exposed.

Scar stumbled into the small clearing and glanced around. "Johnny?"

The Bounty Hunter rose to a crouch and pointed his gun at the outlaw. Though his mind was frazzled, something like a plan formed.

He ducked out from under the brush and pressed a finger to his lips so Scar could see.

"Son of a—"

The huge, blind dinosaur, obviously relying on sound, moved out of the dense foliage.

The Bounty Hunter shook his head and motioned for Scar to follow him as he retreated into the brush. But Scar either did not understand or care. He drew his revolver and aimed it at the Bounty Hunter.

Some men, like Scar and Johnny, the Bounty Hunter knew would never see reason. Some men, you just couldn't reach. A fact he came to realize throughout his life. Some people were just fools. Like Scar. No matter how cunning...

"You," Scar said. His face was sheened with sweat and blood from various small cuts littering his forehead and cheeks. He staggered forward, gun still on the Bounty Hunter.

The Bounty Hunter shook his head and pointed at the monstrous dinosaur's snout protruding from the foliage. Its nostrils flared, no doubt taking in the man's scent. Scar squinted but didn't look to where the Bounty Hunter pointed. Instead, he moved closer to the Bounty Hunter.

"No, you fool," the Bounty Hunter whispered. "It's—"

The monster lunged out of the foliage and scooped Scar up in it jaws before he had a chance to fire a shot, let alone scream. Blood splattered the ground and the massive dinosaur walked away, ground trembling with every footfall.

The Bounty Hunter sat, wiped Scar's blood from his face and watched the creature disappear into all the green of the lost world under the mountains. Scar was gone. Half his bounty was gone. But Johnny was the largest bounty of the two. The ringleader, even though it appeared Scar was in charge sometimes. Johnny had always been the leader. Maybe it was Johnny's plan to make Scar appear to be the leader for whatever reason the Bounty Hunter wasn't sure of.

His body was a knot of pain as he stumbled out of the brush.

He needed to get back to Johnny and somehow drag the bastard out. If the man was still conscious and kicking, though, things could get tough.

The Bounty Hunter found a spot where he could see the red glow of where he left Johnny and began running.

He just hoped he wasn't too late.

23

Whatever got to Johnny must have been ravenous because where his stomach should have been was a large, bloody crater. And whatever it was ate all the way to the spine.

The strength in the Bounty Hunter's legs threatened to buckle him.

A loud roar staggered him.

Something close and didn't sound like the blind dinosaur, or the one with the big head and little arms.

This one sounded different. A bit shrill.

He drew both revolvers. If this was to be his last stand, then so be it. Both his bounties were lost. He could drag Johnny's corpse out, but first, he needed to survive the hellish things coming for him.

The Bounty Hunter planted his boots and waited for whatever may come.

Leaves and brush rustled. The thing behind all the green roared again…and another followed. Then another.

And another…

The Bounty Hunter's heart stuttered. His eyes widened. His grip on the butts of his revolvers tightened.

There was more than one behind that veil of green. But how many?

Most of the leaves trembled now, though not too tall. Maybe about two turkeys stacked on top of each o—

The first thing he killed entering this lost world was about as tall.

There were more of them.

Instead of facing them, the Bounty Hunter turned and ran toward the red glow lighting the vast world under the mountains.

Dozens of shrill roars exploded behind him.

Run, his mind screamed. *Run until you can't run anymore*!

And he did.

Shrieks blasted at him from behind, but he didn't care. He kept running. His focus was on the source of the reddish glow. What he assumed gave the entire vast cavern under the mountains its light. Even the green was tinged with red.

So, he ran and did not look back.

Eventually the shrieks faded and all he heard was deep humming. The ground, the bits of red rock, everything, rumbled under his feet. The motion nearly tripped him up, but he didn't stop running. If he stopped, they would get him. How (or why) they hadn't yet was beyond him. Surely those things could run faster than him.

This thought made him pause stride until he slowed and turned around, guns ready.

A thick stench invaded his nostrils, but he ignored it to make sure he knew what the creatures were doing.

They were following him, but not running. He couldn't tell how many paces away they creeped, but it was far enough he couldn't make out much of their features. Mostly just the silhouettes of their bodies. Though, the longer he stood still, the closer they slunk and the more features he saw. Eyes. Teeth. Claws splayed...

The Bounty Hunter would waste no time shooting them, though he wondered why they weren't attacking him. They certainly appeared like they wanted to. He backed away while keeping his eyes and guns on them.

It didn't take long for the extreme heat soaking through the back of his shirt to draw his attention away from the dinosaurs.

He stopped and turned.

The Bounty Hunter gasped, eyes instantly tearing up. Rumbling filled his ears. He stumbled away, nearly tripping over his own feet and falling. What lay in front of him was an orange and red lake. Steam curled upward into the cavern's upper darkness. The stench, he recognized. Reminded him a little of the dozen or so rotten eggs in their henhouse back home one summer after a fox got into the coop. A thick rotting smell like sulfur. Like hundreds of matches being struck at once in a small room.

The lake itself was too bright to really look at so he spun away and, unknowingly, made his way toward the hungry dinosaurs.

But that wasn't right. Did lakes *flow*? The glimpse the Bounty Hunter managed before the heat and light forced him to look away revealed a vast lake, and yet, it moved. It *flowed* like a river.

He had heard about mountains exploding with fire not long ago, though those were stories he shrugged off. Stories from some southern island. He forgot the name. But he was under the mountains right now, or, rather, within them. Or maybe a bit of both. The reddish orange stuff flowing by was hot. Hotter than any fire he could remember. Enough to make the skin on his face tighten and instantly dry. If he turned fully to the heat, maybe the skin would crack.

Instead, it baked into his back as he moved toward the dinosaurs. They weren't coming any closer now and instead hopped around, front claws splayed and toothy maws snapping and eager. They knew to not get close to the lake of fire. That's why the creatures didn't run after him. They knew he would come back. It was all just a waiting game.

He could try to shoot them, but the distance was too far. His bullets would either fall short or plink off them like hand tossed coins.

The six-foot dinosaurs did not attack, rather, they remained where they were, waiting for the Bounty Hunter to get close enough to take down. The heat at his back lessened and he slowed his pace at the same time they began moving forward.

His heart was a mess of erratic beats. The Bounty Hunter stopped and pointed his revolvers at the creatures.

There were at least a dozen of the things, if not more. How many bullets did he have left? Whatever remained was in the loops of his belt, though he didn't dare look. He needed to keep an eye on—

One of them broke free of the pack and sprinted across the red landscape toward him.

The Bounty Hunter leveled a revolver, keeping it aimed on the dinosaur's head. It still wasn't close enough yet, so he waited. Let his heart ease. Dropping to a knee, he focused on the six-foot dinosaur racing toward him. Close, but not close enough.

Almost fifty yards now.

Thirty.

Twenty...

He waited a few seconds more and squeezed the trigger, sheering off half of its head in a spray of red. It stumbled, though continued toward him. The Bounty Hunter's eyes narrowed. He aimed the gun again and fired. This shot took out most of its head. A pink tongue lashed in the bloody crater that used to be its mouth.

And, still, it ran at him.

"Shit," he said and moved aside just as it rushed by, taloned feet kicking up red rocks.

It ran until the edge of the flowing lake of fire and burst into flames. It barely managed a squeal before the lake claimed it in a flurry of flames and ashes.

In a blink, he was sent sprawling on the red gravel. Pain spread through his upper back. Low chittering sounds filled his ears, even over the rumbling flow of the fiery lake. The Bounty Hunter rolled, guns ready to—

A tail whipped the right revolver from his hand hard enough to send the gun flying toward the lake of fire. He scrambled away, right hand numb and worthless for the time being. He caught a glimpse of something gray shoot by in front of him as he gained his feet.

Sharp pain shrieked from the back of his thigh. He stumbled forward, barely catching his balance. Something cut the back of his leg and—

Another slice of pain screamed from his left shoulder, just above the bicep. All around him the creatures darted. Always moving.

Another small cut parted the skin of his lower back.

They were toying with him now.

The Bounty Hunter fought the urge to drop to his knees. Rather, he spun, caught one of the bastards staring at him, and put two bullets in its chest and one that blew apart the top of its head. The dinosaur dropped like a sack of field corn only to be replaced by another. This one lunged and he shot it through the throat. Blood sprayed, dousing the Bounty Hunter.

Something knocked him onto his side hard enough to click his teeth. He rolled, launching tiny red rocks in every direction, and brought his gun up just in time to smack one of the creatures away before it buried its teeth into his face.

If they kill you, a tiny voice in him said, *Ana will die too…*

Ana.

An image of his daughter's smiling face floated before his mind's eye and a roar erupted from him like never before. A rage so new it frightened and exhilarated him at the same time. An unchained demon let loose to destroy everything in its path.

The dinosaur swung back on him, mouth open, teeth ready to rip him apart. The Bounty Hunter about pulled the trigger, but the creature clamped down on the barrel of his remaining revolver. It tried to wrench it from his grip, but he held on. Even being flung around like a ragdoll, he held on. He had to. The six-shooter was all he had left to defend himself. If he lost that one…

The Bounty Hunter kicked the creature as hard as he could in the chest, narrowly avoiding sharp talons made to slice open prey. The dinosaur grunted. Its mouth opened just enough to slip the gun free. He fired two bullets into its face and whirled around in time to blast another creature. Blood misted the rank, hot air. Sweat streamed down his face.

He reloaded and…

The others made odd yipping sounds and sprinted back from where they came.

The Bounty Hunter frowned, and that's when he felt the ground tremble under his sprung boots. His eyes widened, heart skipping a beat. All his insides seemed to squirm.

Barely over the rumbling of the fiery lake, another rumble. Not as deep, though just as terrifying. More terrifying.

He turned and blinked at the dinosaur with the big head and small arms. It cocked its head to the side, as if in question. With all those teeth, it appeared to grin at him. The gray feathers on the back of its head fluttered from the heat-filled breeze coming off the lake. A heat the Bounty Hunter wanted to move away from. He was starting to feel ill. Mouth too dry.

Water.

Something he managed a bit of but never really indulged in since entering this lost world. When you are running for your life, however, necessities like water get tossed to the wayside. He had some water earlier, but not nearly enough.

He glanced around for his other revolver...and his heart sank. It lay a couple of feet from the dinosaur's large taloned feet. Blood seeped from between long, sharp teeth and dripped off the creature's lower jaw. The rifle shot must have done some damage then.

Good.

Still, the thing didn't appear to be phased by it, nor acted injured. It lowered its big head while it still cocked from side to side sporadically like...well, like a bird. A crow, perhaps, while it measured up its meal.

The Bounty Hunter aimed his only gun at the creature. "You ate my rifle, you son of a bitch."

The dinosaur paused, as though it understood what he said, then let loose a roar so loud and forceful he slid a few inches backward, throwing off his aim. The shot went wild and the creature lunged.

He leapt aside before those massive jaws could clamp down on him, whirled and pulled the trigger. The bullet struck the space between the outer corner of its eye and the gray tuft of feathers. It hissed and swung away.

The Bounty Hunter dashed forward, grabbed his revolver from the ground and backed away, closing the short distance between the dinosaur and the lake of fire. He didn't have a plan, but he had both guns back now and, as he backed away, a bit more courage leaked through his veins.

The dinosaur roared and came for him. All teeth and thunder.

There was no time to aim and the lake of fire burned at his back. The heat was getting to him and it took all he could to lift the guns.

"C'mon, you ugly bastard."

The creature sprang forward, mouth gaping. A cavern of teeth.

The Bounty Hunter leaped to the side a second before the dinosaur's massive jaws snapped shut. It shrieked, skidding through the red gravel. But its momentum was too strong.

The dinosaur slipped into the lake of fire.

The Bounty Hunter crawled away from the heat and fire. Coughing, vision blurring.

He crawled back to the forest.

24

He blacked out at some point, but when he returned to the here and now, he was lying on the yellow sand of the beach.

Tiny ripples of water kissed his outstretched fingertips.

The Bounty Hunter groaned and dragged himself through the sand to the water. Once he was partially in the lake, he slurped down some water. Just a little bit to wake his body up. He knew not to drink too much right now. He waited to the count of sixty and drank some more. The water washed over his sore, beaten body, cooling it and soothing all the cuts.

If the forest region were the badlands, the vast area of tiny red rocks serving the lake of fire were the true badlands.

After a few more drinks from the lake, the Bounty Hunter gained enough strength to stand. He swayed and wondered what other horrors waited on the other side of the lake. Not that he would be going that way, just curiosity.

He turned to the forest, then to the lake of fire.

He needed to get Johnny's corpse and leave.

***

Surprisingly, Johnny's body wasn't eaten. Just a bloody crater where his stomach should have been.

The Bounty Hunter untied the body, slung it over his shoulder, and hurried into the forest.

The way out wasn't far, from what he could remember. He needed to find the stream and follow it north. Or what served as north in these badlands. This lost world under the mountains. If any of the six-foot bastards came after him, he would die. There was no way he would have enough time to drop the corpse and take them all out before they pounced and tore him apart.

If the creatures were around, though, they didn't attack.

The forest stood silent. Not a bird, nor any other creature stirred. The only sounds were of the Bounty Hunter rushing through dead leaves and thorny brambles that ripped holes in his grimy jeans. He thought it odd, but, then again, his sole focus was getting to the exit and leaving this lost world far behind him. Get out, get gone, as his dad used to say. That bastard.

Sweat dripped from the tip of his nose, but at least he was sweating and didn't feel so ill. He stepped into a small clearing. It looked familiar, though it could just be his mind playing tricks. He glanced around, trying to gather his bearings and wait for something to pop out at him. A fallen tree or something.

Nothing did, though, so he pushed forward.

The forest was eerily quiet. Not a breeze rustled the leaves.

The Bounty Hunter kept moving. He pushed himself to run faster. Hopefully one of the outlaws tied their horse up, otherwise it was going to be a long, treacherous haul down Arizona Territory way. Unless Warlock didn't run off. And how much would Johnny rot between now and then? No matter how much the Bounty Hunter tried to keep his body cool…from…

Slight sniffing sounds cut through his thoughts.

He stopped walking and turned. His gaze swept over all the green. The sniffing sounds stopped. Somewhere close, a stick snapped. The Bounty Hunter's heart whip-cracked against his ribs. But he couldn't see anything through the veil of green foliage.

Just your head playing tricks, he thought and turned back around—

Its muzzle hovered less than two feet above him.

He stumbled away, nearly dropping Johnny's corpse.

Large, slanted nostrils flared, sucking in air and blowing it out. Slow. With a purpose other than breathing. Its head swept from side to side. Eye sockets, filled with congealed blood, revealed no emotion.

It swung its elongated head back and forth. Its nostrils flared, taking in his scent. It knew he was there but couldn't find him.

Stay still, he thought. *If you don't make noise…*

The muzzle of the monstrous dinosaur stopped moving and once more pointed at the Bounty Hunter. He glanced from the dinosaur to the body he carried. It smelled the blood. Like any predator, it was attracted by the blood.

A thick growl shuddered through the teeth of the monstrosity.

The Bounty Hunter did the only thing could think of.

Run.

He darted to the left, as best he could with a corpse, and ran. The ground soon sloped downward, slowing him a bit so not to stumble and go rolling down the slight hill. He found himself in a dim hollow. It took him a bit to gather himself, but when he did…he spotted the dead dinosaur. The very first one he encountered entering these badlands. It lay in the weeds, just beyond the small stream, head canted at an impossible angle.

The Bounty Hunter jumped over the stream, wincing at the weight of Johnny igniting slivers of pain all through his beaten body. The exit was just up a ragged slope of rocks. A hole in the side of a lost world which should have never been discovered.

Only a few more feet.

A tree crashed down about twenty yards to his right. A branch caught one of Johnny's boots and peeled it off.

The Bounty Hunter, heart practically blasting a hole through him, climbed the rocks to the ragged hole between worlds.

He shoved Johnny's corpse through the large hole and was about to crawl through too when—

A soul shattering roar froze him in place. He turned his head just enough to see the monster dinosaur lunge, mouth wide open.

He pulled himself through the opening before the creature's teeth found him. The monster slammed itself at the opening over and over while the Bounty Hunter moved Johnny's corpse away. He drew his revolvers and stood in front of the hole. If it broke through...if it got free...

So many people would die.

The Bounty Hunter glared at the creature through the hole between worlds and thumbed hammers back on his guns. "Time to put you outta your misery, ol'hoss."

The massive dinosaur shot forward, plunging its mouth through the opening and knocking the Bounty Hunter back into the stone wall. He dropped to a knee, more pain piling onto what he already dealt with keeping him down longer than usual. Hot breath blasted him.

The monster's muzzle was no more than a foot away. It shifted back and forth, though not much. The mouth opened about two feet and snapped shut again. A thin whine filled the air as the creature tried to wiggle its elongated mouth out of the ragged opening. Cracks in the rock snaked to the ceiling. It wouldn't take long before the monster broke through.

Heart stuttering, the Bounty Hunter dragged Johnny out of the cave.

The cool air of the outside world he left behind kissed his sweat-slicked skin. A horse he didn't know neighed. No sign of Warlock. He threw Johnny's corpse over the back and, upon looking for rope, came across a couple of satchels. He reigned the horse down and checked the satchels. One side held three large corked brown liquor bottles with a gray tinged string sprouting from a hole out the top of a cork. Inside was a strange mixture of liquid and something solid. Gun powder, mayhap?

The Bounty Hunter didn't know for sure, but, judging by the gray string, he guessed it was a bomb. The string being something like twine rubbed with gunpowder. Which one of the Ramsy brothers men made it was also a mystery.

A heavy snort from the cave. The crumbling of rocks.

How long before the monster broke free and let loose horror onto the territories?

He hefted the bottle. The liquid sloshed around inside. He turned to the cave. All he needed was a match. Flint and steel. Something to light the makeshift fuse. A quick check of his pockets and his heart sank a bit. Somewhere along the line, he had lost his stick matches.

He searched through the pockets of the bodies on the ground (Apple?) and found a neat box of stick matches.

Luck, he thought, and ran into the cave.

Already the monster had broken the opening wider. Its jaws opened wider and snapped shut with a loud *thunk.*

The Bounty Hunter struck a match and lit the gray fuse of the bottle bomb. It took no time for the spark to surge over the midpoint. He waited for the monster to open its mouth again and when it did, he threw the makeshift bomb inside.

He made it about ten paces when the explosion shoved him forward and knocked him to the rocky ground. A constant ring invaded his hearing. He rolled onto his side, gasping. The bomb was much more than he thought it would be. Smoke and the stench of charred meat polluted the air. Coughing, he dragged himself out of the cave only to collapse near the horse.

As everything faded to darkness, something shrieked.

25

The shrieking brought him back.

How long he'd been out, the Bounty Hunter didn't know, but the air stank of burned things and full of shrieks so loud he had to cover his ears while he rolled onto his side. Everything hurt.

Once all the hurt and confusion subsided, he sat up...and blinked.

It was not a mouth sticking through the ragged hole anymore, but a large, steaming, mangled clump of charred and pink flesh. Only a few teeth remained on the top jaw. The cave smelled like the chicken legs he burnt by accident the first time on his own. A whine floated out of the ruined crater of smoldering meat and teeth.

The Bounty Hunter sighed and walked back to the horse. He brought out both remaining bombs and stared at the cave's entrance while the monster cried.

He soon mounted the horse and moved closer to the cave.

Eventually the monster would die. Other things would feed off it. It would rot and fall away, leaving the hole open for anything curious enough to climb through and into this world and time.

Sometimes...things were just meant to be left in the past...

The Bounty Hunter tied the fuses of the bombs together, lit it, and tossed them both into the cave. Wincing at all the pain roiling through his body, he quickly turned the horse around and galloped away with Johnny's corpse flopping across the back of the stallion.

The explosion wasn't as loud as he thought and only a few crows cawed in irritation. He stopped the horse and turned. Because he needed to make sure. He needed the closure.

Once the dust cleared, he gave a nod, turned south, and rode into a dawn of a new day.

The cave was sealed. Worlds once more shut of each other.

Lives could go on, though he would never forget the lost world under the mountains, the lake of fire.

He would never forget the badlands.

BETTER DAYS AHEAD

The Bounty Hunter hadn't ridden far before a familiar neigh caught his attention.

He pulled on the reigns to stop the horse and turned in the saddle until he spotted the black shape racing toward him.

Again, the familiar neigh. A sound which struck him instantly and wrapped him in warmth. Tears filled his eyes at the sight.

He smiled and wiped a tear from his bruised face. "Hi, old friend."

Minutes later, he unstrapped the saddle and let the stallion run free.

Warlock nuzzled his back while he watched the other horse wander away. The Bounty Hunter chuckled, turned and gave his horse a good petting.

"Love you, pal."

Warlock snorted and nuzzled the Bounty Hunter.

***

Time passed, and for the Bounty Hunter, it was time well spent.

"Do we have enough wood?"

The Bounty Hunter nodded and lit a rolled cigarette. He leaned back in the rocking chair and watched the flames dance over the chopped logs in the fireplace. Outside, a blizzard for the ages raged.

If he hadn't forced the sheriff of Springwood to pay the five-thousand-dollar reward for Johnny's corpse, they might be so well off right now. All it took was a couple nudges from the Bounty Hunter's revolver to get the old man to cough up the reward money.

"Food?"

Again, the Bounty Hunter nodded and smoked.

"It's going to get cold."

He chuckled, leaned back in the chair and looked at Ana. "We are just fine, my joy."

Ana stopped wringing her hands and nodded. She paced a bit, then sat down in one of the chairs near the fire.

"Are you sure? Last winter, Elizabeth ran out of wood and—"

"Ana," he said with a smile. "This winter will be the warmest of all. You will never go away from the table hungry. I promise."

The fire crackled in its place.

The Bounty Hunter smoked his cigarette.

"I love you, Daddy."

He turned back to her, and smiled. "And I love you, my joy. Always and forever."

The back door opened, letting in a gust of cold and snow before it slammed shut and locked.

"Got the wood covered in skins," Michael said, unbuttoning his buffalo hide coat. "Should be dry for us after the storm."

"Many thanks," the Bounty Hunter said. The boy had grown some since he first met him. Taller now, lanky. More articulate and a good worker with an even greater heart.

The Bounty Hunter pointed at the fireplace. "Hot stew over the fire, there. Get yourself a scoop."

While Michael did just that, Ana said, "Will you have to go out again? Will you leave us?"

The Bounty Hunter, taken aback, glanced from Michael to his daughter. Her eyes were wide, nearly pleading.

"We have enough now," he said, finally. "There is no need for more."

Ana let out a long breath of what he assumed was relief.

"However," he said, "if we are in severe need, I will have to collect more bounties."

She sucked in a sharp breath, as if he slapped her, though eventually nodded.

"You will not."

The deep voice took the Bounty Hunter off guard for a second or two.

Coy stepped into the room and hunkered down near the Bounty Hunter's chair. He looked at the fire, then at the Bounty Hunter. His eyes sparkled in the flickering light like polished diamonds.

"You are done with that life," Coy said. "It is time to love. Time to rest."

The Bounty Hunter smiled, nodded and looked back at the fire. He watched the flames, red, orange, yellow, blue. He watched them dancing and wondered if the Devil was looking right back at him.

All those sins…

He smoked his cigarette and watched the flames dance.

THE END

Check out other great
Dinosaur Thrillers!

Gustavo Bondoni
TEST SITE HORROR

Lieutenant Max Alexeyev is a Russian Special Forces soldier. His job is to protect his country's interests at home and abroad, not to rescue overly ambitious reporters who have bitten off stories too big to chew. But when his unit gets called to a press event at a laboratory that has been invaded by dinosaurs, that's exactly what he finds himself doing. Fighting both prehistoric nightmares and the products of modern genetic experiments in the forests of the Ural Mountains, he battles for his own survival as well as that of alluring journalist Marianne Caruso and her peers.Unbeknownst to him, however, shadowy human forces are at work to ensure that no one spills the secrets of the research being done in the area.Will they live to tell the story of the Test Site Horror?

John Lee Schneider
AGE OF MONSTERS

Once upon a time, Dinosaurs ruled the Earth.But the Mesozoic era – the Age of Reptiles – came to its cataclysmic end sixty-five million years ago.The Age of Monsters begins tonight.And the world of humankind will crumble. Some will call it Judgment. Some will attempt to fight. Others will simply run. Most will just try and survive. But no one will escape.In the mountains. In the oceans. In the cities and towns. Even up in space.Where were YOU when the world ended?

Check out other great

Dinosaur Thrillers!

Doug Goodman

HUNTING WITH DINOSAURS

A hunting party is sent to catch and kill raptors that have escaped Dinosaur Falls Restricted Area and murdered nearby hikers. But the hunters find the raptors are unlike any creature they've ever hunted, and soon one lone bowhunter is running for his life through the Perdidos Mountains. He discovers an old wilderness survival trench and burrows in deep, but eventually the raptors come for him. His only salvation is to befriend a wolf hellbent on destroying the raptors. If they can come together, they can form a pack the world has never seen, but if they fail, the raptors are waiting with their sharp teeth and elongated claws...

Edward J. McFadden III

DINOSAUR RED

There's a doorway on Mars that has mankind's greatest minds perplexed. Deep beneath Aeolis Mons an ancient secret is revealed, and a team of explorers led by Forest Judge, Deputy Commander of Gale Base Alpha, are dispatched to investigate. The prehistoric gateway reveals a biosphere preserving Earth's distant past, and as Judge and crew stand on the threshold of mankind's greatest discovery the Martian ground trembles. A roar thunders from within, the doorway closes, and the team is trapped. Six mission specialists, each with unique skills, each with different reasons for wanting to break free of the primordial trap. To get home Judge is forced to choose between escape and changing the course of humanity. What will he do?

Check out other great

Dinosaur Thrillers!

Greig Beck

PRIMORDIA: IN SEARCH OF THE LOST WORLD

Ben Cartwright, former soldier, home to mourn the loss of his father stumbles upon cryptic letters from the past between the author, Arthur Conan Doyle and his great, great grandfather who vanished while exploring the Amazon jungle in 1908. Amazingly, these letters lead Ben to believe that his ancestor's expedition was the basis for Doyle's fantastical tale of a lost world inhabited by long extinct creatures. As Ben digs some more he finds clues to the whereabouts of a lost notebook that might contain a map to a place that is home to creatures that would rewrite everything known about history, biology and evolution. But other parties now know about the notebook, and will do anything to obtain it. For Ben and his friends, it becomes a race against time and against ruthless rivals. In the remotest corners of Venezuela, along winding river trails known only to lost tribes, and through near impenetrable jungle, Ben and his novice team find a forbidden place more terrifying and dangerous than anything they could ever have imagined.

William Meikle

THE LOST VALLEY

A remote high valley in the Canadian Rockies hides an ecosystem that has been lost in time. A small team of prospectors and their local guides are looking for gold. What they find is blood and terror and death. The valley's monstrous inhabitants are not about to let go of its secrets lightly.